STARTED FROM A SELFIE

NICOLE FALLS

SILENT N PUBLISHING

ACKNOWLEDGMENTS

nic's nook aka the best reader's group in the land: i luh y'all for real.

obi wan penobi: you stay listening to me whine about these fictional folks and never block me. you da bess! thanks seem insufficient. forever indebted.

all of my friends: y'all are everything. i love you.

mama and papa: y'all are more. i love you.

[redacted] family descendants (both sides!): your support as i endeavor to build this new career is astounding. couldn't have asked to been born into a better clan. i love you all.

I WAS RUNNING LATE. I absolutely hated running late, but when I went out to my car this morning, and it wouldn't turn on? And my sis and bruhbruh were MIA? I had to make a quick decision. So, I left the car and walked the ten minutes to the train station, so I wouldn't be later than I already was. I shot a quick text to Joey to let her know that I was running behind.

Real people behind or Juju behind? - Joey the Great

I giggled at her response because she always teased me about my need to be super on time for everything to the point of arriving up to thirty minutes in advance of a meeting. One of the things my mother ingrained in me and my sisters was the importance of timeliness. She always said that being late was a form of disrespect. The lack of attention to other people's time showed that you held them in low regard, and it's something I've carried with me from a very young age. Having to reroute my morning would have me getting to the client's house just before our appointed meeting time, but to me, that was still late.

I texted back to let Joey know that I was behind by my own standards, but perfectly on time by anyone else's. She just laughed and agreed to pick me up from the train stop for the quick ride over to our client's house. The little side hustle that my best friend Jonique and I started on a whim was beginning to pick up steam. What started as a silly throwaway joke at Jojo's monthly girls night had evolved into a website, blog, and workshops on demand. We were hanging out with some college friends, and one was complaining about never being able to cum via penetration. It was causing a bit of strain within her relationship, and she was legitimately put out about it. I, of course, immediately began asking all sorts of questions to see if this was onset with this partner or if it had always been this way for her. And that led to all the women in the group talking about hardly ever being satisfied when engaging in sexual intercourse, which made me hella sad.

Sex is amazing, but if not done right can seem like a chore. These women, myself and Joey withstanding, were going on and on about their lack of fulfillment by their men (and women, in one case) in the sack. A quick poll of these women brought the shocking result that none of them owned sex toys and only three of the seven had masturbated before. I finally blurted out, "You hoes need to mind your own pussies! How are you supposed to know what brings you pleasure if even you don't know your pussy intimately?" After a stunned silence and the uproarious laughter that followed, we went from sitting around shooting the shit to having an impromptu conversation about sexual expectations, pleasure zones, and body exploration. Many of these women's first sexual experiences were at the hands of inexperienced teen boys who were undoubtedly more concerned with getting theirs than making sure anyone else in the room was satisfied.

After chastising them for not knowing themselves enough to know what they liked, I gave each of them homework to spend some time exploring their bodies and after that, to initiate sex with their partners taking what they'd learned from their self-exploration into consideration. Within a week all of them had reported back with positive results, and many of them suggested that I share what I'd told them with the masses. I told them that there were more than enough sex bloggers out here, but they all insisted that I brought something to the table that was unique. All of them kept bringing it up to Joey, insistently and Jonique—practical planner that she is, hit me with a full-on PowerPoint presentation outlining the pros and cons of doing this thing. I'd never been one to back down from a challenge, and Joey presented sound logic, so "Mind Your Own Pussy" was born.

Today we were on our way to facilitate one of my favorite workshops, "Rockin the Mic" at a private home. The woman who coordinated the workshop was a friend of one of Jojo's friends and had been reading the blog. She thought it would be a fun diversion for her and her girlfriends as well as a means of getting more education on ways to please her man. Celena had been comfortable enough to express to me, while setting up the workshop appointment, that while she felt her man was adequately satisfied, she was looking for tips and tricks to blow his mind—no pun intended. I assured her that once we were done today, she'd be armed with everything she needed to make her nigga say uhhhn na na na na, like Percy Miller n'em.

About halfway through the train ride, something in the air shifted. Suddenly, I was keyed up and didn't know why. I looked around the train, slightly on alert, trying to figure out where this charge in energy came from when my gaze landed on the finest brotha I'd seen in a while. He was the possessor of smooth skin that looked like whipped peanut butter, shoulder length, jet black locs, and a beard so lush that it looked like a soft place to lay all of your burdens down. Gahdamn, I muttered to myself, garnering a "mmmhmmm girl" from the older woman who was sitting next to me. I giggled at her reaction and sent a quick text to Joey.

My future baby daddy is on this train, bih. I might not make it.

IKYFL. - Joey the Great

Remember that IG personal trainer nigga we were stalking that was posted on wreckmyuterusplz? Think him, but like...finer.

Pics or it didn't happen. - Joey the Great

I laughed again, louder this time because Joey swore that whenever I was describing something to her that she wasn't there to witness that I was exaggerating. This was no exaggeration though. The way that the cutie and I were positioned, it would be mad obvious if I aimed my camera in his direction to try to snap a shot. So instead I turned my phone into selfie mode, pretended to be searching for the right light and snapped a shot that had him perfectly framed between the edges of my hair and one of those poles for standing on the train.

OH BIH. - Joey the Great

Told. You. Finer, right?

I officially give you permission to blow this work-shop off and blow that young man's mind. Report back with details. - Joey the Great

I cackled once again, garnering the fine dude's attention. Our eyes locked for a quick second and I smiled, hoping that looked like an invitation for him to follow up. You see...for as much bravado as I possessed when it came to talking with my homegirls or the MYOP clients and followers, I never actually approached men. Call it old-fashioned—or cowardly—but I was typically very lucky in that when I showed the littlest chance of being open, men generally took advantage and made their way to me. Mr. Fine offered a smile in return and nothing more. Quickly my eyes shot downward to his hands, making sure that my first cursory overview didn't miss a ring, but nope there was nothing there. Oh well, probably somebody else's guy, so that little fantasy was ruined.

No dice. I'll see you at the Cottage Ave stop, sis.

Did you even try? - Joey the Great

I smiled at him.

Seriously, Juju? SMH. I am disappointed in you. *eye roll emoji* Do better! - Joey the Great

Joey knew my deal and her teasing was all in good fun. She did have a point though, maybe I needed to hop out of my comfort zone and approach him. I could do this—had done this for several friends in the past, so it shouldn't be anything for me to conquer for myself. I blew out a breath, rolled my shoulders a few times and steeled myself to get up and move in his direction. When I looked up, however, he was gone. I whipped my head back and forth looking around the train and it was almost as if I made him up because he was nowhere to be found. I navigated back to my Photos app to make sure he wasn't a complete apparition. I looked at the photo, zooming in on him and grinning like a loon. But I also noticed that I looked cute as hell in the pic, so I decided to upload it to the gram with the caption "out here looking cute and mah future baby zaddy in the back zont eem notice...". My stop was the next one, so I put my phone away, gathered my supplies and prepared to disembark the train.

"Ok ladies," I said, clapping my hands to get their attention as I addressed the group, "you should have been given some homework from Celena prior to us gathering here today. Who wants to go first?"

"Cel, baby girl, did you really think this through when you decided to put this together? Do you realize how often we see each other and our significant others? I don't need to remember that every time I see Reem that he's especially fond of you lapping at his dick head like a dog in a water bowl, like, really boo?" a woman whose name I think was Raquel said.

The entire room fell into laughter, Joey and I included. This wasn't the first time this concern had arisen in one of our workshops, but I wanted to set everyone at ease quickly.

"Ladies, we won't be sharing these things aloud from the source," I started before holding up a pad of paper and a hat, "You're going to write down the answers to that question I told you to ask your men and then we'll go through these anonymously and talk through any tips and tricks that anyone in the group has to offer before going into the hands-on portion of this workshop. So, don't worry, you won't have to avert your gaze too hard because you won't know who likes what...but hell depending on how freaky these answers get, you might be unable to even look your homegirls in the eyes at the end of today."

That set off more laughter and let me know that we would be working with a good group here. None of the women seemed uptight or uncomfortable, which was always crucial to ensure a successful workshop. Having even one woman who wasn't with the program could sway the mood of the entire room and had, in the past, led to some very tense workshop sessions.

Joey went around passing out the slips of paper and pens for the women to write on, while I went about setting up my computer for the presentation portion of the workshop. It was surprising to me the number of people who were grossly misinformed about the basic anatomy of the male and female sex organs, so every workshop started off like those "how your body is changing" seminars that everyone attended in elementary school when puberty was jumping off. I tried not to drag out the anatomy lesson for too long but always found it helpful as we segued into the meat and potatoes of the workshop.

So far, we had three workshops that we offered: Rocking the Mic—our male oral sex workshop, Snack Chat—our female oral sex workshop and P in V—our co-ed intercourse workshop. Rocking the Mic was our most popular, by far, mostly put together for groups of friends or family or sorority sisters as a part of their bachelorette festivities.

"All right ladies, let's get the boring part over

with, so we can get into why y'all really wanted us here today," I said, launching into the first slide of the presentation.

There was a moment of tension midway through when the neighbor of the hostess, Miss Rita, abruptly interrupted Joey explaining how that whole grapefruiting thing from Girls Trip wasn't something they came up with on their own.

"Little girl, I've probably been sucking dicks longer than you've been alive, why are you giving us an oral history, no pun intended, of dick sucking? Let's get to the good part!"

You could have knocked Joey over with a feather after that interruption, and the rest of us were honestly no good for the rest of the session. A couple of hours later, my abdomen hurt from laughing so much. This session had definitely been one of our liveliest, with the ladies having no filters and little regard for boundaries as we discussed tips, tricks, and techniques for sucking dick. Joey and I even learned a couple of new things that we would be incorporating into future workshops thanks to Miss Rita. As we wrapped up, I shared business cards and our social media information with the ladies so that if they had referrals, they could quickly pass them our contact information.

We left Celena's house, grabbed a quick bite to eat and had a debrief session before Joey, saint that she is, drove me home so I wouldn't have to make the trek on the train again. It wasn't an enormous imposition, but the time saved by getting a ride home as opposed to having to take the train gave me a bit more time to decompress before joining my sisters for dinner at Ginger's. I loved all of my sisters, but Gigi definitely tried my patience of them all. She was such a control freak, and it drove me insane. She tried to act like my mother instead of my older sister as she criticized my career choices, lack of a stable mate, and the fact that I still lived with our oldest sister in our childhood home. Gigi tended to mind everyone's business but her own which drove me batty. Nono and Lolo usually ignored her when she got into high drama mode, but for some reason, I didn't have that ability. Every comment, no matter how innocuous, always set me on edge. I'd been working not to let her take me there, but not even an hour-long session with What's Going Om? before heading to her house was good enough to keep me centered.

I walked into the house to see my sister Noelle and her guy Jay all cuddled up on the sofa.

"Hey, Junie B.," Noelle called out as I shut the door behind me.

"Hey, No. Hey, Bruhbruh."

"How'd your session go today?" Noelle asked.

Noelle was the only one of my sisters that knew about Mind Your Own Pussy. She was amused when I told her about Joey and me going into business together with this idea. Lolo likely would have been amused as well, but I could just see Ginger's face screwing up with that "I just ate a lemon" look before she launched into a speech of condemnation.

"It went really well, actually. One of the girls who was there knew you. Said y'all went to West together. Her name was Patty, I think?" I said, pulling out my phone to pull up the group pic so I could show Noelle who I was talking about.

My sister was great with faces but terrible with names. As soon as I showed her the photograph, she recognized her immediately. Patty had recognized my last name and asked if I had a sister named Noelle and launched into reminiscing about their days on the tennis team in high school. She said they were like the Bring It On squad, a cadre of black and brown girls rolling up, playing predominantly white schools and, racking up Ws left and right. I'd completely forgotten that Noelle played tennis in high school because she did so many other things in addition to that. That was my big sis though, Miss Popularity, a definite hard act to follow.

All of my sisters were hard acts to follow, really. It was hard growing up as Baby Girl Holliday because almost every school official and teacher I came into contact with expected me to be super gregarious like Noelle or quietly brilliant like Lolo or take charge and decisive like Gigi. Meanwhile, I just wanted to be Juju. In trying to make a name for myself beyond their shadows, I became a hodgepodge of the previous three. Eventually, though, I figured out who Juju was and was currently having fun being irreverent, but not belligerent me.

I sat talking about the workshop with Noelle and Jay for a few minutes more before retreating to my room with Noelle's promise to wake me up in ninety minutes so that we could drive over to Ginger's together. Also got Jay to promise to have my car towed to his homeboy's shop for the freeski so they could check it out and hopefully not charge me too much to get it back running.

"DADDY, ARE YOU LISTENING TO ME?" my daughter whined.

"Yes, Junie, I am, but that doesn't mean you're going to get your way," I responded knowing damn well that she was going to get her way.

We were in the mall, at her insistence. In Finish Line, also at her insistence. We were allegedly just coming in here to see how this pair of rose gold 11s looked on her feet, not for her to try to talk me into spending damn near $200 on a pair of shoes for the second time in a few months. She'd already gotten me for a pair of the Season of Her Js that she just had to have. Because I was a sucker and her mother was immune to her charms, she knew this little trip would end up working out in her favor.

"I thought we were supposed to be bonding, baby girl," I said before signaling to the kid hovering not too far away that he could ring me up for the shoes.

His eyes lit up at the thought of the commission as I ran my fingers through my locs with a sigh. This little girl had gotten me once again. I was just glad she was actually willing to hang out with her old man, even if it was under the guise of bonding that was clear manipulation. I'd heard of most little girls becoming nightmares for their parents as soon as the clock struck twelve on the year in which their ages ended with teen, but so far—three years in— Junie was still my darlin' baby girl.

She turned to me wearing the sweetest smile and replied, "We are bonding, daddy. And rather splendidly if I do say so myself. I mean my love language is receiving gifts, and you just bought these for me, so I'd say we are killing the daddy-daughter bonding thang in these streets."

I couldn't do anything but laugh as she removed the shoes from her feet, placed them in the box and we walked toward the cash wrap. The aforementioned salesman already had us all rung up, and he was just waiting for me to insert my card and sign to complete the transaction. After we finished ringing out, and that lil nigga had the audacity to try to flirt with my baby girl in front of me, we headed over to Junie aka Quincey Junior's favorite restaurant, Wildfire. She was clearly all about going deep into my pockets tonight, but I wasn't fazed. We were celebrating because, for the sixth semester in a row, my girl had brought home an all As high honor roll report card. As long as she kept working hard and bringing home all As, I had zero problems spoiling her, much to her mother's chagrin. But Charity had learned to stop trying to regulate how Junie and I bonded pretty early on. She insisted that I spoiled Junie, but I countered that I was just rewarding excellent behavior. The problem was that money was no object when it came to my baby, but Charity was so damn frugal that trying to get something extra outta her was like squeezing blood from a turnip. Since Charity was the full-time custodial parent, Quincey Junior to had to deal with her tightfisted ways for a long while until she learned that she had me wrapped around her baby finger and started using her powers of manipulation for good.

Both my mother and Charity consistently reminded me of how much of a sucker I was and also said setting Junie up for unrealistic ideas of what it meant for a man to be in her life, but they were trippin'. My baby had every right to be expected to be treated like royalty because that's what she was (no hotep) and she needed to remind every single one of these knuckleheads out here that if they couldn't put in the effort that her pops put in that they might as well hang it up.

"Dang, daddy, your phone is blowing up," Quincey said, as we drove over to Wildfire. I'd left my phone in the car while we were in the mall and came out to it buzzing nonstop. I picked it up to see who was trying to get in contact with me, but the screen was filled with a bunch of notifications from Instagram, which was strange. I only had an account to keep up with the moves Junie was making online, so I had no idea why my notifications would be going off crazy style. Whatever it was could wait, however, because nothing was more important than spending time with my baby girl.

Much of dinner was spent with Junie filling me in on the goings-on in her school life and the lives of her friends. On the one hand, I felt honored that she was comfortable enough to talk to me about her peers, but if I had to hear one more so funny story that wasn't that funny at all, I'd be ready to dig my eardrums out with the salad fork. After dinner and to-go dessert, we were headed to drop Quincey back off at her mother's house with intentions of picking her up in a few days, so we could travel to go see my parents who had moved South to avoid the harsh winters of our home state. As I was dropping Quincey off, my phone rang, and according to the dashboard, it was my boy Ant. I should have known better to answer the phone through the car with Junie sitting here, but I went ahead and answered it anyway.

"Aye nigga who is this fine hoe that tagged you on IG callin' you her future baby daddy?"

"Say what?" I asked.

"Bruh, Bree tagged me in some girl's photo asking if it was you she was talkin' bout in the caption. Shorty is bad as fuck, bruh. If you ain't getting on it, I am definitely bout to slide head first into them DMs like ay yooooo."

"Hey Uncle Ant," Quincey chirped.

"Aw shit, dawg. I forgot you had Junior with you tonight. Hit me later, nigga," Ant said, hanging up before I could respond.

I guess that's what those Instagram notifications from earlier were about, I thought as I picked up my phone to investigate whatever Anthony was talking about. Before I could navigate to the app though, Quincey had grabbed my phone from my hand, protesting against me texting and driving. Instead, she let me unlock the phone while she did the Instagram investigation. Navigating through my notifications to the photo in which apparently tens of people had tagged me, Quincey came upon the picture in question. We were stopped at a light when she turned the phone so that I could view the photo. As soon as I saw the photo, a grin spread across my face as I remembered the absolutely breathtaking sista who had almost made me miss my damn stop on the train this morning as I tried to covertly check her out while not seeming like a creep. As keyed into her as I was, I was shocked that I didn't even remember seeing her phone being out, nor that she was taking a picture in which I was caught in the frame.

"Ohmigod daddy, my new stepmommy is gorgeous," she squealed, damn near bursting my eardrums, "You totally gotta slide in her DMs before Uncle Ant does, daddy. You want me to send her something?"

"Pass me my phone, little girl. Stay in a child's place," I said, trying to sound stern, but failing miserably from laughing.

"One sec, daddy," Quincey said, before handing my phone back to me.

When I looked at it, I saw it was still on the picture of the beautiful stranger, but my eyes immediately locked onto a new comment posted in the thread from me that was simply the emoji eyes.

"Really, Junebug?"

"Aw c'mon daddy. Where's your sense of adventure? I know you and Sheila aren't together anymore and this lady...she's a glo-up, daddy. Especially compared to Sheila."

She tried muttering that last line under her breath, but I heard her loud and clear. Sheila was an on again, off again...friend of mine. I hesitated to give her the title of the girlfriend because she and Quincey Junior never managed to get along. At first, I thought Junie didn't like her because she wasn't used to seeing me around any woman who wasn't someone to whom we were related, but I soon discovered that Sheila had a very conde-scending way of dealing with my baby girl. And, while she and I had no beef, I couldn't abide by her and my baby beefing. So, when it came down to it? Sheila had to be dismissed.

"So, you drop the creep eyes? Damn, you couldn't make me even slide into her DMs like a re-spectable thot?"

"Daddy, please. One, you're not a thot. You're a catch. And secondly, you gotta make your interest known publicly. You didn't see the rest of those thirsty ni...men with comments talkin' about what they would do to her since you were so oblivious."

"You're a little too invested in this Junebug. What's that all about?"

"I just...daddy's gotta have a life too, right? Mommy and Chuck have been married for years, but the only person you were remotely halfway se-rious about was unsuitable and unstable."

"Damn, baby girl tell me how you really feel?"

"I'm just saying, daddy. This Juju lady could be The One."

"And what exactly do you know about The One, young lady?"

"Enough to know that you've been ducking and dodging her like you owe her money. It's been time for you to settle down, daddy-o."

"You're killing me here, kid. But if she is The One, that doesn't explain why you got me out here on my creep steez?"

"Leaving it up to you, your corny behind would have slid into her DMs mad proper on some 'excuse me queen...' notep adjacent mess. I'm keeping you current, old man."

"Yeah, yeah...tread lightly, lil girl."

Quincey flashed her trademark, double dimpled grin and winked.

"I'm just sayin, daddy..."

After dropping Quincey off, I headed home to unwind and catch the last couple of games in the season before NBA playoffs. My boy Russ was on the verge of averaging a triple-double for the second season in a row, which was insane. That man was a beast, easily my favorite active player in the league. Tonight, he and OKC were taking on the Grizz. I got home, grabbed a brew from the fridge and plopped down on my couch ready to settle in for the night when my phone chimed with an unrecognized tone. I picked it up to see if that shorty replied to the comment that my presumptuous child saw fit to send. Nothing from her, but there was another interesting reaction to that photo that made me navigate from Instagram to my texts.

You callin' me a bum ass baby daddy?

My phone chimed with a response immediately.

Calm down, negro. I just warned the girl not to let the pretty face fool her. - Case

Damn, it's like that, baby mama?

You changed my name from Charity Case in your phone yet or nah, baby daddy? - Case

I chuckled because in a fit of petty when I felt like she had her hands out a bit too much beyond the court ordered child support that I was paying, I'd changed her contact info to read Charity Case instead of her government name of Charity Jacobsen. I eventually got over it but jokes trump facts, so I kept her in my phone simply as Case. It became a nickname of sorts, much to her chagrin.

Touche. You ain't have to blow up my spot like that tho.

Yeah yeah, whateva. You'll be aight. - Case

I hesitated before sending my next message. Although Charity and I had been together officially for less time than it took to gestate Junior, but we did have our fair share of...difficulties before we got to our current state of peaceful co-parenting. Admittedly, I wasn't the best father...or man for those early years, giving both my baby and her mama the runaround as I tried figuring out who the hell I was. We got pregnant with Quincey at a young enough age for me to still be out in the streets looking for the next best thing but at an advanced enough age that I should have gotten my shit together immediately and manned up. It took a few years, but eventually, I got it together. Those years of game playing, however, led to a massive amount of strain between Case and me that had honestly only been resolved in the past few years.

...so you know shorty?

Really, Q? You that hard up that you need your baby mama to hook you up? - Case

Nevermind, Case...

I'd just have to get to know more about her on my own.

━━

"Aye bruh, you j down on shorty yet or nah?" Ant asked as soon as I emerged from my car.

We were out at Pembroke Park for an early hoop session before I had to head to the shop for the day. Initially, I was supposed to be off today, but I decided to pick up a few extra hours to offset the unexpected extra money I'd spent on and put into Junior's pockets.

"Good morning to you too, Anthony," I replied with a chuckle.

"Nigga, since when are you Miss Manners? Did you slide or nah? Coz if it's fair game..."

"Now you know damn well Nina would beat your ass—again—if you even thought about tryna slide anywhere but right beside her ass on the couch to watch this week's episode of Scandal. Relax."

Ant gave me the middle finger but didn't refute my claim. He and Nina had been together as long as Junie had been on this Earth and this negro still kept tryna play games with her like he was really going somewhere. Despite sticking with Ant this long, Nina had no desire to tether herself to him permanently by means of marriage, and as much as he hated to admit it, I knew it had him tight. So, Ant would talk mad shit about leaving her and finding someone else, but he never exactly seemed to follow through on any of that talk. And all this talk about him sliding in ol girl's DMs was nothing but that...talk.

"So you tellin' me you ain't said shit yet, got it," Ant replied, dribbling and throwing up a quick shot.

The ball bounced off the rim, and I snagged it from mid-air, dribbling a couple of times before throwing up a shot of my own.

As the ball cascaded through the net, I said, "I said something...well...kinda."

"What's kinda nigga? Either you did, or you didn't."

"Well..." I hedged and told him about Junie leaving the comment under the photo on my behalf.

"You know, you really need to establish some firm boundaries between you and Junebug, Q. You got your daughter shooting your shot for you? And you let a weak ass emoji be the only thing you said? Wow, I thought I taught you better."

"Excuse me?"

"You heard me. I know after you finally got rid of Sheila's clingy ass you got on your eat, hoop, work shit, but bruh...it's time. And shorty is wide open. Nigga, she called you zaddy...you know the shit is real when they spell it with a z. Do better."

The earnest look of disappointment on Ant's face made me break down laughing.

"Man, you so ignant. Eat, hoop, work, really?"

"The nigga equivalent to that white lady's search to find herself. Great film, honestly. You should watch it, you could learn a lot," Ant deadpanned.

"Why do I even talk to you?" I asked, shaking my head.

"Because beyond your mama, Charity, Junior, and Jesus, I'm the only one who'll put up with your moody ass."

"Man, whatever, we hoopin', or you wanna stay in the feelings circle a little longer?"

"Check up, nigga."

After a couple of games of one on one, we parted ways, and I headed home for a quick shower before heading down to Holt's. I hadn't been working there long, but so far, so good. I was referred to this job by my boy Prentiss who was the operations manager. The shop that I'd been working at unexpectedly shuttered, Prent came through right on time with this opportunity. I was still in my probationary period, but I definitely saw myself at this joint for the long haul. Unlike the shop I worked at previously, this one had a good group of guys that I didn't mind being around for up to twelve hours a day, some days. The owner, Karim, ran a tight ship but was also a fair boss. He'd stepped back from the day-to-day operations a lot, leaving Prentiss to make sure things flowed smoothly. And as a former Navy guy, Prent definitely kept us running like a well-manned oiled machine.

When I walked into the shop today, it was quiet...despite loud ass Darrell being on the schedule for the day. I nodded to him before heading to the back to put my stuff in my locker and change into my coveralls. I checked the work orders and saw we had a relatively light day ahead of us so far, with a couple of oil changes and a busted starter that needed to be repaired. I had grabbed one of the oil changes to get started but was stopped by Prentiss and told to attend to the car with the starter issues since it was a VIP, and the owner of the vehicle was due to be picking it up in a few hours.

I SAT LOOKING at my phone, gaze homed in on the notifications screen at the one comment I'd had no clue would even appear nor was I sure how exactly to respond to it. Let me back up, first of all, I did not expect for my silly caption to be noticed by so many people nor did I expect for any of them to actually tag the object of my affection in the damn comments. Weren't these people aware of social media etiquette? It totally dictated that unless I expressly tagged someone, I didn't need anyone else tagging that person for me. Of course, I set myself up for this by being silly in the first place, but that was unimportant now. What was important was how I would respond since not only had everyone and their mama tagged this man, but he'd also essentially left it up to me to make the next move by leaving those damn emoji eyes. And what did those eyes even mean anyway? Was he interested? Annoyed? Taken aback? Ugh, this whole thing was just stupid.

I put my phone down and laid my head down on the counter next to it. I was at an advanced enough age to not be trippin' over something as simple as initiating contact with a man. If I could sit in a room of thirty women and describe in painstaking detail the quickest way to get their man hard and ready, I certainly could slide into this man's DMs with something witty or hell, not even necessarily witty considering that he'd left a damn emoji in response.

"Argh," I growled, remaining frustrated.

"Morning, Junie B," Jay said.

I popped up, heart racing, clutching my invisible pearls. I was certain that he and NoNo had stayed at his place last night, so his sudden appearance just scared the shit outta me. I honestly didn't know why they kept playing themselves with this separate residence mess when it was clear that they were on the path to wedded bliss. It was only a matter of time before he popped the question, they said I do, and I'd be solely responsible for the bills in this house. I was incredibly happy that Jay and No found their way back to each other, but sometimes witnessing their saccharine evolution left me feeling...a bit left out. Noelle and I were the last two single Holliday sisters, and now that she and Jay were coupled up, that left just me. And I faced zero pressure to be couple up, but I'd be damned if being the 7th wheel wasn't hella awkward.

"Hey, brudda, good morning. I thought y'all were next door."

"We were, I actually came over to talk to you," Jay replied, sliding onto the stool next to me at the breakfast bar.

"What's up?" I asked, figuring he had details about my car that his homeboy was working on.

Jay said nothing, reaching into his pocket and

retrieving a small item that he placed on the bar in front of me. I looked down to see what it was and gasped.

"So we are finally doing this?" I exclaimed, hopping up and down as best as I could while seated.

"You don't think it's too soon?"

"Boy quit playin! This has been like forty years in the making, man! Hell, I thought I would get married before y'all two fools finally saw the light. Hell, no this isn't too early. It's right on time."

Jay grinned, rubbed the back of his head and let out a breath.

"I don't know if she's ready though. She's going to say I'm moving too fast. You know your sister!"

I said nothing in return, just reached for the ring box to take a look at what he was working with. Opening the box, I immediately let out a low whistle as I looked at the ring. It was gorgeous and hella Noelle. A simple round cut pink diamond with a delicate, filigreed rose gold band. I lifted it out of the box to inspect a little more closely and noticed an inscription on the inside and felt myself tearing up after reading it. The inscription on the inside of the ring read *"From 12.19.98 until forever"*.

"I do, in fact, know her. Better than you, bruh, and trust me she isn't going to say anything but hell yes. This ring is incredible. You did good, brudda. Real good."

"Yeah?"

"Negro, please. You know this ring is everything. How do you even remember the exact date of when y'all first moved in tho? I can barely remember what I had for lunch yesterday," I laughed.

"How could I not remember the first day I met

the woman I would love forever?" Jay replied, a hint of disbelief in his voice that I would question him about that.

"So when are you gonna do it? How are you gonna do it? Where are you gonna do it?"

"Do what?" Noelle asked, scaring the shit out of both Jay and me.

Jay recovered quickly, covertly scooping the ring box and placing it back in his pocket before making his way to wrap Noelle in an embrace.

"Mind your business, Yes," he replied, dropping a kiss on her forehead.

"You are my business," she countered.

"Touché."

"So are y'all gonna tell me what you were talking about?"

Jay and I looked at each other and answered in unison, "Nope."

"Both of y'all suck. Just for that, I'm not making breakfast."

"Yes you are," Jay replied, easily, "You promised after I did that thing with my..."

"HEY! OK! Child in the room here," I yelled, popping up from my stool.

They both just laughed and paid me no attention as they moved into the kitchen so that Noelle could cook. Seeing them together just reminded me of the damn set of emoji eyes sitting in my notifications that I had no idea what to do with. An emoji reply...really my guy? He totally could have given me something to work with here instead of a pair of googly eyes.

"You know you're overthinking this right?" Joey laughed at me after my ten-minute rant about leaving emoji as a response instead of using your words, "You could just send him a hey whassup hello and call it a day instead of doing whatever this is."

"Wow, I thought you were on my side," I replied.

I was being dramatic. I knew it. Joey knew it. But neither of us was supposed to acknowledge the facts of it all. It was an unspoken rule of our friendship. Or so I thought.

"I'm on the side of whatever makes the best story. Besides, you know you could have just asked him what he meant by the damn emoji when you slide into his DM, sis. You've been sending yourself into a tailspin unnecessarily this whole time. What is this? I mean I know you have your hang-ups, but this...this feels...different."

I could tell by the tenderness that crept into her tone that Joey was genuinely trying to figure out what my deal was and to be perfectly frank, I didn't even know where to begin with an explanation.

"Jo, I don't even know, sis. I just don't even know," I replied, sinking my head down into my up-turned palms and sighing.

"So, are you gonna ask him what it meant or are we going to table this discussion until after we retrieve your car from Holt's?"

I made a non-committal sound, shrugging, "Isn't that too lame though? Why is this so hard?"

"Girl..." Jonique sighed.

"I know...I know. Let's just...lemme grab my jacket so we can go get my car."

Luckily, there was nothing seriously wrong

with my car. It ended up being a short in some wiring or something, but easily, and more importantly, economically reasonable to fix. Joey came over to drive me to get the car since we had another workshop to facilitate later in the evening and we needed to go over a few new details we'd added to the presentation. Instead of doing that, however, I'd pulled her into my web of ridiculousness in which I analyzed a damn emoji from every possible angle. When I came back downstairs, Joey rushed me out of the door, refusing to make eye contact.

"What's going on, Jo?"

"Nothing," she replied a little too quickly, which let me know that something was definitely up.

"So, we're choosing to serve the Lord with lies on today, sis?"

"I just wanna make sure we get your car and don't end up being late is all. C'mon."

I looked at my watch, noting that we had a smooth two and a half hours before we actually had to be to our workspace which was right around the corner from the shop where my car was being serviced.

"Girl...just let me grab my phone then we can roll."

"I got it, here..." Joey replied, holding it aloft from her position near the door, "Can we go now?"

"Why do you have my phone?"

"Because I was being efficient?"

"You don't sound too sure about that. What did you do, Jo?"

"What makes you think I did anything?" Joey asked, her normally smoky voice sounding decidedly squeaky, which was the first clue that she wasn't telling the truth. Joey was the worst liar, and her voice went from late night soul to Brittany the Chippette whenever she wasn't telling the truth.

"Because you sound like you have sisters named Eleanor and Jeanette right now. So, I'm going to ask you again, what did you do?"

"I mighta kinda sorta slid in lil buddy's DMs for you?"

"Jo."

"Ju."

"You know I hate you, right?" I said, walking over to snatch my phone to see what she sent.

"I love you, too, boo," she replied, blowing a kiss in my direction.

I rolled my eyes before locking up and following her to her car so that we could get over to Holt's. As soon as I settled into the car, I opened up Instagram to see what the hell Joey sent this man whose name I still didn't know.

Message sent to @qdagr81: so do those eyes mean you're interested in going half on a baby with me or nah?

QUINCY

I'D JUST WRAPPED up checking the car I was working on to make sure it would start with no issues when my phone buzzed. Before I could pull it out of my pocket to check it, Prentiss approached asking if I was finished with the job I was working currently because the owner of the car was up front. I let him know that I was gonna give the car a quick vacuum and wash, but that shouldn't take more than ten or so minutes. I figured since it was a VIP client, we should be giving the full service, red carpet treatment. Approximately, eight minutes later I pulled the car around front, reentering the service center waiting area to return the keys to its own.

The waiting room was half-filled, although most of the folks in the space weren't paying me any attention as all eyes were on the television screen. There was a breaking news story about an active hostage situation. The task at hand momentarily forgotten, I too turned my attention to the television as the newscasters gave details about the family who was currently being held against their will by an embittered ex of one of the household's members. The news reported that there were currently negotiators trying to talk the gunman down to prevent any casualties. I wondered what it took to get someone to that point. That had to be some next level punani, I thought, shaking my head. Presently, I got back to the task at hand, looking down at the work order to call out the customer's name for the car I'd just finished servicing.

"Juniper Holliday," I called out.

There was a moment of no movement before two women got up headed toward me. They started heading toward me when suddenly the one in the back, grabbed the one leading the way toward me and started whispering furiously. I leaned back on the counter awaiting their approach when familiarity suddenly struck. She was wearing a baseball cap, so I hadn't recognized her immediately, but the woman in the back was shorty from Instagram. Dressed down, she was still bad as fuck. She was dragging her feet until her friend forcibly pushed her ahead and damned near into my arms. Caught off guard by her friend's sudden movement, the woman lost her footing and was on her way to the ground. I was leaning on the counter but moved forward to help brace or avoid the fall. I misjudged honey's speed because the next thing I knew we were both sprawled on the ground, with her planted firmly on top of me.

"Oh my god! I'm so sorry," she exclaimed, hopping up immediately with a hand out trying to help me up.

I brushed her hand off, bracing one of my own

against the floor, before pulling myself up. Since she'd come at me full force and I was caught off guard, I was a bit slower to get up.

"No worries, sweetheart," I replied easily, "I assume one of you is Juniper?"

"Mmmmhmmm, her," the friend said, shoving Juniper into my direction again, "But there's no need for formalities, future baby daddy. Friends call her Juju. But I'm sure you already knew that."

Juniper turned toward her friend scowling and muttered something that sounded like a threat of an ass beating, but the friend just laughed it off.

"Your car is right out front," I replied, holding out her keys.

Juniper grabbed the keys and made a beeline for the front door while her friend moved at a slower pace before turning back to face me.

"So, does that mean you're not tryna go half on a baby with my sis or nah?"

"Excuse me?"

"You're the guy, right? From the IG photo. I saw the spark of recognition in your eyes, so I know you know who she is. So whassup? Are you otherwise engaged? Or disinterested?"

"I..."

"I mean, it can't be disinterest because a- she's fine as fuck and for two, you were practically drooling when you realized who she was, so..."

Before I could even attempt to respond, Juniper stuck her head inside the door, "Jonique Latrice Langford, you have three seconds to bring your ass."

"Relax, sis. I'm coming," the friend who I now knew as Jonique replied.

She pulled out a business card, placing it in the

pocket on the front of my coveralls and said, "Look, I don't know what's what, but if you're interested in my girl—take the shit offline. Our office isn't far from here. Come through, mack her down the old school way."

I chuckled, "Seems like your girl is the one who ain't interested. I was zaddy on the internet, but she couldn't get outta here fast enough today."

"You caught her off guard, without her armor. Trust me. She's interested."

I chuckled, "Aight, bet. Good look, Jonique."

"Friends call me Joey."

"Joey," I acknowledged with a head nod.

"I'm serious, don't be a stranger!" she replied before strutting from the building.

Through the door I could see the two ladies fussing back and forth, Juniper gesticulating wildly as Joey calmly laughed. The exchange was no more than ninety seconds before both jumped into their respective cars and peeled out of the parking lot. I reached into my pocket, pulling out the business card that Joey had placed there. I thought that it was her card, but it was Juniper's, replete with all her various means of contact from business address to email to phone to social media handles. Flipping the card over, I looked at the logo before letting out a loud laugh. Emblazoned in a purple circle were the words "mind your own" and an emoji cat whose eyes were replaced with hearts. I pulled out my phone to navigate to the website on the business card to figure out what kind of business these two ladies were running exactly.

There were a few notifications of texts and other apps, but I cleared those and opened up a new Safari window, typing mindyourownp.org into the search bar. Their site loaded quickly, and I navigated to the about page. In a few concise paragraphs, the ladies gave the history about the genesis of their business, a sex-positive service based in teaching women about their bodies and sexual satisfaction. Both ladies were certified sexologists—huh who even knew that was a thing, I thought. I was so caught up in exploring their website that I hadn't noticed that Prentiss had snuck up behind and was reading over my shoulder.

"Rockin' the Mic? Now you know yo ass is too old to even think about becoming a rapper, Q?"

"You should mind your business, old man."

"I got your old all right," he replied, muffing me in the head, "Get your head out the clouds and back to work, fool."

I laughed, shoving him away from me and heading toward the back to complete my next work order. The rest of the day moved at a glacial pace since there wasn't much to do. Prent actually ended up letting a few of us go a little earlier than anticipated since there was nothing more for us to do than to sit around looking at each other's ugly mugs. NBA Playoffs had officially started, so a few of the guys decided to go to For the Love of the Game to grab some brews and catch a game or two. I accompanied them since I wasn't about to do anything but go home and do the same thing. We decided to just walk over to the bar since it was pretty warm out. On our walk, we ended up passing the Mind Your Own...workspace and damn near being run over by a group of pretty ass women who were exiting. They were so caught up in their conversations that they didn't even notice us grease monkeys walking through. Darrell tried spitting some weak ass game but was quickly shot down when all the women flashed their ring-covered hands as if they were background dancers for Beyoncé. The rest of us laughed, giving him shit for being unobservant and super thirsty as usual.

The bar was unsurprisingly packed, but we managed to grab a table near the end of the large bar, close to the kitchen. After taking our food and drink orders, the server scurried away quickly, looking uncomfortable by the way Darrell was leering at her.

"Rell...I'ma say this one time, and then I'm done," I started, "You gotta stop being such a creep, my man. You gotta know that shit ain't attracting any honeys. And I don't need them thinkin' we all creeps by association, bruh."

Larry and Will nodded in agreement. They were sick of his mess too and usually didn't even bother inviting him out with us because we didn't wanna deal with the backlash.

"Everybody ain't a pretty boy with hoes sweating them on social media, Q. I do what works."

"Negro, please. It never works. Ever." Will replied, laughing.

"Aww, don't be sad, Rell," Larry broke in, "Someday your prince will come."

"Fuck you, nigga," Darrell replied, making us all break down in laughter.

"Man, just how small is this town tho? You saw that Instagram shit, too?" I asked, "Shorty actually came in the shop today."

"Word? She a stalker type?" Darrell asked.

"Total coincidence. She seemed pretty low key. Her homegirl was a lot though," I laughed.

"Hook me up?" Darrell said.

"Nigga," Larry, Will, and I said at the same time, laughing.

"So what up with it, Q? You finna get at shorty?" Larry asked.

"I...ionno, man. We'll see."

They all just looked at me and shook their heads, mumbling various versions of "this motha-fucka" under their breaths. I'd already decided that I was gonna hop down on Juniper as soon as I'd gotten a free moment, but that wasn't any of their business. Don't get me wrong, these dudes were cool to work with and even grab a brew or two with, but I swore they gossiped more than women. If I gave them any inkling of my plans for getting to know Juniper, it'd be the topic of discussion in the shop until Rell did something stupid to make everyone forget they were discussing me and mine. At the rate Rell did dumb shit, it likely wouldn't have been more than a couple days, but more than a couple minutes of discussing my personal life was more than I cared to share with these cats.

<hr>

We were in the Uber to the airport in the wee hours of the morning, but that didn't stop Junie from being a chatterbox the entire time. Apparently, there was a scandal because Miko's cousin saw Miko's boyfriend and somebody else from their friend group all hugged up in somewhere...the de-tails were fuzzy because I, admittedly, tuned out about forty-five seconds into the conversation.

"Can you believe that, daddy?" Junie asked, bringing me back to the present.

"Nah, baby girl, that's crazy," I replied by rote, having zero ideas what she was referencing.

"I know you weren't listening, old man," Junie smirked, "So let's talk about something that does interest you...how's my new stepmommy?"

"Junior...please."

"Did you make her take down that picture, so the thirst buckets could stop replying?"

'Little girl, what are you talking about?"

"She deleted the pic!"

"How do you know?"

"Because I kinda sorta maybe cyberstalked her a little. But in my defense..."

I said nothing, motioning for her to continue, but silence reigned in the Uber.

"Your defense...?"

"Ok, I really don't have one, but daddy..."

"Mind your business, Junie."

"But--"

"Quincey...mind your business."

The bass in my voice shut her up quickly, a muttered, "Fine then, be forever alone" was her only rebuttal. I let that slide because I might've deserved it. The fact of the matter was the rest of my work week got crazy, so I couldn't slide over to her place of business with lunch as I'd planned. Then it was time for Junie and me to head down to Arizona to visit the folks, so my plans of the in-person mack down, as her homegirl had put it, had been effectively squashed.

I'd spent the past four days getting double teamed by my daughter and mother about still being single and never giving Junie siblings and my mother a "proper daughter-in-love". Thankfully, Junior had kept her mouth shut about Juniper in front of my mother because I could only imagine how that would have gone. It was bad enough I had to endure her trying not so covertly to set me up with every single woman from age twenty to fifty-five that she knew. And my dad was no help as he passively sat by and let my mother get away with her shenanigans. Secretly, I think he too was jonesing to be a grandpa again because all that free time of retirement gave him and my mother a bit too much time to sit around the house looking at each other, and both welcomed any sort of distraction from their normal day to day routines. Damn shame when a man can't even count on his father to have his back.

"Ok, I know you told me to mind my business, but can I ask one question, daddy?"

"Nope."

The Uber driver barely stifled a laugh that let me know she'd been listening to the duration of our conversation, despite trying to act like she wasn't paying us any attention.

"Daddy!"

"You already know too much, little girl, so whatever question you have is gonna violate you minding your business as I kindly asked you to, so...nah, you can't ask just one more question."

Quincey pouted, huffing and blowing out a breath while crossing her arms over her chest. She sat there with her lip poked out looking all of eight years old, instead of nearly sixteen. It was nearly cute enough for me to give in, but Ant was right. I did need to establish boundaries with Junior. I spent too much time treating her like my lil road dog, giving her too much information about me and how I move that she didn't need to be privy to. She'd get over it soon enough, hell it had been a long time in the making anyway.

"Fine!" she huffed once again.

"Yo, relax. You're doing a lot right now. You're not too old to get embarrassed," I ground out in a low tone that made Quincey sit up immediately, uncrossing her arms and turning to stare out of the window.

We made it through the rest of the ride and TSA with the kid remaining quiet. Even my attempts to make conversation with her by asking about her friends or if she wanted something to eat or drink were met with nonverbal responses. It wasn't until we were taxiing on the runway, damn near ready for takeoff that she spoke again. I'd already settled in with my headphones playing some classic JayZ when Junior tapped me on the shoulder. I paused the music, turning toward her to give my undivided attention.

"I know you told me to mind my business, but I'm just gonna say this one thing, and I'm done. Don't you ever feel like something is missing, daddy? I mean, I know you have me, and I'm the best thing that's ever happened to you, but beyond that what else do you have? Work, that's boring. You don't have hobbies. And your friends...I love Uncle Ant, but he isn't exactly...anyway, I just think that if you had somebody, not even saying it has to be that Juju lady, could be anybody, you'd smile a hel...ck of a lot more and stop being so freaking uptight all the time. I really am just looking out for your happiness, daddy. You deserve," Junior finished, and without awaiting a response, pulled her wireless beats over her ears and leaned over to snap a few photos of our view from the clouds.

The kid might've had a point, but I'd be damned if I let her know it. I would, however, plan to make getting to know Juniper priority number one as soon as we touched back down in the City.

JUJU

"TELL me again why you can't come today, Joey?" I asked, exasperated.

We'd been slammed with workshop requests lately and that had taken its toll on my good sis. I could barely hear her when I answered the call and had her switch over to FaceTime to finally understand what was going on. Her voice was completely gone. Laryngitis according to the fine folks at the Minute Clinic thanks to the paperwork she'd flashed across the screen when I accused her of faking it.

"Ju," Jonique croaked, her barely audible voice nearly unrecognizable.

"Okay, sorry," I laughed, "I'll stop giving you a hard time. You good, though? You need me to bring you anything?"

Jonique scribbled quickly on the notepad she'd grabbed to make our conversation go quicker.

I'M GOOD. THX 4 ASKIN BOO. SRY :-)

"It's fine, sis. I mean there was gonna come a time where we would have to split off and do these on our own anyway, right? I've done Rock the Mic so many times; I could prolly do it in my sleep. Don't worry."

That sent Joey back to scribbling on her notepad. She flipped it up with a smirk settled on her face as the words she'd written sank in for me. I'd assumed that today's session was a Rock the Mic workshop because it was our most popular as well as most often scheduled. Today, however, was a Snack Chat—my least favorite to facilitate, not because of content, but because people that were signed up for this one usually fell into one of two categories. Men who were signed up against their will or lesbians who thought they wrote the book on minding the gap. Both groups brought with them a sense of entitlement and standoffishness which undoubtedly led to tension throughout the entire session.

Joey, bless her spirit, usually let the tension roll right over her as she burrowed through the lesson and practical applications, but the way my me was set up? I carried the stress of it with me for the rest of the day. And considering how my former favorite means of stress relief was no longer available due to a cross-country move and smashtastic breakup? I would definitely be heavily reliant upon relaxation means number two after the session. I looked around my room to make sure I had my pen and it was full for when I came back home. Joey, omnipotent unicorn that she was scribbled onto her notepad once again.

I have an extra cartridge if you need it. :-)

"Yep, I do need it and I'll stop by you on my way to...aw man, this is a private workshop too? Damn, I thought it was at MYOP. Yep, I'll definitely be hitting you up before making my way over to this

Quinny Finley person's place. What an odd name, Quinny...I know, I know I'm one to talk named Juniper."

Joey said nothing, just laughed soundlessly. I rang off with her and got back to what I was working on before she had called. In addition to running MYOP with Jonique, I also ran my own web design business. What had started as me being bored on the internet and playing around with HTML and CSS eventually evolved into being self-taught and self-employed. I started with making websites for people I knew, and word of mouth helped launch my fledgling business, much like the evolution of MYOP, only this wasn't one that would get me a side eye from my mama and second mama, Ginger. I set an alarm because I tended to get caught up in designing that I lost track of time and tended to tune everything else out. And I was working on a site for a friend of my sister's who was launching a skincare line that involved some pretty heavy responsive coding, so it would be nothing for me to get lost in that and run right up to the time I needed to be in my whip and headed to my appointment.

I drove through a side of town I didn't have cause to visit often, caught up in the vibrancy of the neighborhood. For years, most of my childhood and early adulthood, this side of the neighborhood was run down and on the verge of ruin, but a revitalization project initiated by a few hometown heroes had really turned this area around. Where there were once boarded up greystones, was now a beautifully composed neighborhood that looked the way the founders likely imagined it would look after their passing. I turned the radio down as the GPS informed me that I was less than a quarter of a mile from my destination. Joey always made fun of me for turning down the radio like that would help me read the address numbers more clearly, but I low key thought it did help.

Soon I was pulling up to a greystone with an immaculately kempt lawn and rose bushes that were in the early stages of bloom. I grabbed my things from the trunk, carefully stepping onto the walkway to avoid the kids running and playing back and forth along the sidewalk. I took a couple of minutes to take in my surroundings instantly transported back to my youth. Despite living in the same house, my neighborhood had changed drastically. We had no kids on our block and I'd kinda missed the sounds of kids running roughshod over the block, living their best lives. Shaking off the memories of years well passed, I rolled my suitcase up the sidewalk and short porch before I rang the doorbell.

"It's open," I heard a deep voice intone.

I opened the door, rolling my suitcase in, instantly on alert because it was very quiet when I walked in. I flicked my wrist up to take another look at my watch, confirming that while I was early I wasn't so early that I would make it here before the rest of the party.

"Up here," the same voice that told me the door was open sounded again.

What a rude ass, I thought, while I lugged my suitcase up the short flight of stairs that led to the second floor of the greystone. It wasn't super heavy, but damn was chivalry dead these days? A gentleman would have offered to help me with my things. I rolled my eyes and steeled myself to be met with resistance as soon as I crossed the threshold of the door. I walked into an apartment beautifully decorated in cool grey and navy, with spots of lush greenery placed strategically in the living and dining areas.

"Hello?" I called out.

"You can set up in the den, straight through the kitchen to your right," a voice called out from near the back of the apartment space.

Oooookay, I said to myself rolling my bag into the indicated space and immediately beginning set up. After a few minutes, I was all set, but the owner of that deep rumbling voice had yet to reveal himself, nor had any other guests shown up for the workshop. I knew sometimes folks were operating on CP time, but if no one showed up within the next ten minutes, I had no problem issuing a refund and hightailing it the hell outta here. I played around on my laptop a little, getting the Power-Point set up when I suddenly felt a twinge of...something.

I looked up to see that handsome, peanut butter skinned, freshly twisted loc god I'd embarrassed myself in front of both in virtual reality and real-life reality.

"I-It-It's...you..." I stammered.

Real cool Juniper.

He walked over with a hand extended, reaching out to encase mine in his.

"I don't think we've ever actually been formally introduced. Quincy Finley, my pleasure to finally, officially make your acquaintance."

I damn near swooned out of my shoes, but

quickly recovered introducing myself, "Juju Holliday. Um, Quincy...where's the rest of your party?"

"Party?"

"Yeah, you booked a workshop. That's usually
facilitated by me for a group."

"Oh, I thought we could have a little one-on-
one action if you don't mind," he replied, flashing
me that panty wetting grin.

It almost had me before I his words really per-
meated my brain.

"One on one?" I asked, "That's not really a
thing we offer."

When MYOP first started we had more than a
few creeps contact us thinking that we were offering services that were less of a sexologist and
more in line with prostitution. Our mailbox was
overrun with dick pics, improper solicitations, and
indecent proposals. For the most part, we'd been
able to weed out a lot of the bullshit, but every now
and again one slipped through the cracks. They
never, however, tended to make it any further than
my personal guard dog aka Joey.

"Not even for a possible baby daddy," Quincy
asked, that smirk still gracing his handsome ass face.

I rolled my eyes, "Unbelievable. Of course,
you're trash. That's right in line with my life right
now. What a waste of fine. No, we do not offer any
one on one services, you creep."

Angrily, I shut my MacBook and began
throwing things into my suitcase haphazardly.
Quincy reached out, grabbing my arm trying to halt
my progress, but I shrugged him off continuing to
get things in the bag so I could get the hell out of
there as soon as possible.

"Yo, sweetheart, chill, it's not like that."

"It's not like what? Not like you booked a whole workshop about eating pussy under the guise of getting me here alone in your apartment to do what exactly? Not like you deliberately misrepresented yourself to gain favor? Not like you manipulated this whole situation and put me in a potentially unsafe environment? Tell me, Quincy, what isn't it like?"

Not waiting for an answer, I rolled my bag back toward the front of the apartment to move straight out the door, back into my car, and home when I was stopped by Quincy trying to grab me by the arm once again.

"Negro, you must be out of your cotton pickin' mind! Get your hands off me!" I said, forcefully shoving him away from me.

"Juniper, please, give me a minute to explain. This isn't what it seems like, I promise," Quincy pleaded.

Something in his voice, a thread of sincerity laced with a bit of disappointment caused me to turn my eyes back upon his face. He looked like he'd seen a ghost, regret clearly etched across his features—hands up in the air, palms stretched wide like he didn't want any problems. I said nothing, truncating my stride and resting a hand on my hip.

"So...I now see that this looks shitty. Like, really shitty. But in my defense, I thought you'd find it charming. I mean you did ask me to go half on a baby and all," he laughed, but I remained unmoved, "I meant no harm, honestly and understand if you want to go. But do know I expected nothing more than us being able to spend some time together, in person; maybe get to know one another a little better. The only reason I chose the 'pussy eating' workshop as you called it was because there was no way in hell I was booking shit called Rock the Mic and I thought the P in V one would have definitely been the creep move."

At that I had to crack a smile, he did have a point. He had chosen the less creepy of the three options. That didn't exempt him from still choosing the creepy way out instead of the normal way. Also, he was out way more money booking this workshop than he would have been if he'd just asked me out the old-fashioned way. If Twitter ever got wind of this, they'd debate themselves to death about a $500 non-date.

"You couldn't just...ask me out like a normal person? I mean, damn, you had my contact info, man."

He shook his head, biting his lower lip, properly chagrined, "I know, I wasn't thinkin' clearly."

"Clearly!"

"Damn, can I live?"

"Nah, not yet," I replied, with a grin, slightly loosening the grip I had on my luggage and my key ring with the mini spray can of pepper spray attached, "The rules say I get to roast you for at least ten more minutes."

"Fair enough," he acquiesced, before taking the few steps to close the distance I'd put between us, "But...can I try to make it up to you?"

The combination of his adorably sheepish grin, combined with his thumb rubbing circles on the top of my handmade it virtually impossible for me to say no. Not that I was fighting hard against his charm anyway. Initial misinterpretation aside, so far, he'd been nothing but respectful and hadn't shown me anything that would warrant me needing to remain on alert.

"That depends…"

"On?"

"Does making it up to me include food? I'd kinda counted on snacking over the course of the workshop."

Quincy chuckled, a sound that instantly warmed me.

"That could definitely be arranged."

QUINCY

JUNIPER WAS JUST COOL. Very down to Earth and—once she realized that I wasn't trying to force myself upon her—chill as hell. I was used to women who were two handfuls, with lists of demands and standards that were a mile long. Not to say that she was devoid of any of that, but tonight we just vibed. What I had initially thought of as an ingenious idea, was quickly proven to be the opposite and I'd almost fucked things up with her completely. Luckily—due to nothing more than The Man Above, honestly—she gave me a chance to not only speak my piece, but also make it up to her for the misunderstanding, which led to us being where we were currently, sitting on opposite sides of the couch on my back deck, debating which 90s girl groups could or could not sing.

"Quin. Cee. You cannot tell me that you're putting XScape over SVW? I can't believe I'm sitting in the house of a man who would dare utter that phrase, for one, and utter it with confidence, on top of that? Tuh!"

"So you gon sit up here and act like 'Off the

Hook' didn't slap? Like the big girl wasn't singing for her cornbread on Who Can I Run To? That's what we're doing today? Wooooooow."

"Sir. Sidechicks with Voices had multiple albums that slapped. Plus, Coko could sing all four members of XScape under the table while having an asthma attack. You're buggin'," Juniper said, "Wait...this is the true test of just how trash—"

"Or amazing," I broke in.

"Or amazing," she conceded, "your music taste really is. Going strictly off vocals, not who had the most songs that slapped or which ones you thought were finest. Solely by voices—TLC or EnVogue?"

"That's an unfair comparison," I said.

"Just answer the question, man. It's not that hard. I gave you the parameters that set you up for there to only be one answer," Juniper quipped, leaning toward me, eyes narrowed.

"So, you obviously want me to say EnVogue, but —" I started, toying with her because they were going to be my answer all along.

She held up a hand before I could continue, "I'ma stop you right there, pleighboi. The answer is most certainly EnVogue. Now if we wanna talk about who had more heaters, then I might have to put my undying love for Terry Ellis' upper register to the side and begrudgingly admit that TLC has them bested in that category."

"You real serious about your 90s girl groups, huh?"

"I'm really serious about everything. A hazard of being the youngest, most of my life has been spent fighting for the right to not only have an opinion but to have it be heard. And in a house full of women, tuh! Yeah, I learned early to make my opinion known—loud and strong," she replied with a touch of something I couldn't quite place in her tone, "Besides, no use having an opinion, if you don't feel so strongly about it that you'll argue it to the death, am I right?"

"So, in the spirit of that frame of mind, you know I'm not letting this XScape versus SWV discussion go away, right?"

"As long as you can accept that you'll forever go down on the wrong side of history," she trailed off with a grin, "Hey."

"Is for horses."

"Oh my god, shut up," she said, playfully slapping my arm.

That slight tap brought my awareness to our level of proximity now. We'd been keeping our space, on opposite ends of the couch, but somehow during the course of our conversation, we had managed to converge near the middle of the couch. The lull in conversation gave me an opportunity to ogle just how fine Juniper really was openly. She was casual as hell in a long dress that buttoned all down the front, but still effortlessly fly in an unassuming sort of way. My eyes roamed her face, committing every single part of it to memory—from the tiny, nearly imperceptible beauty mark near the left side of her hairline to the barely visible dimples in her cheeks that only appeared when she smiled or smirked to the lush set of lips that were covered in a deep berry-colored lipstick prior to our meal and the wine that had accompanied that meal. Her lips now bore the stain of indulgence after a couple of glasses of Tempranillo.

Her deep-set, almond-shaped eyes seemed to bore through me as our gazes caught and held for a couple of beats before she cast them downward, biting her lower lip.

"You look like you want to kiss me," Juniper said suddenly, "You do, don't you?"

Initially, I said nothing, momentarily taken aback by her forwardness. One thing I should not have been surprised by as she'd had no problem saying what was on her mind for the duration of our conversation all night. When they were handing out filters, Juniper must've been busy getting back in line for second helpings of fine because hers was nonexistent as far as I could tell. She was irreverent, but never crass or disrespectful.

"I do," I replied after a couple of beats had passed, "But I'm treading lightly. I mean, I did almost get pepper sprayed earlier after a misunderstanding. Didn't wanna risk it a second time."

"You shook?"

"I'm cautious. There's a difference."

"I don't bite...unless that's what you're into."

Juniper laughed at my raised brows and moved in a little closer, her dark brown orbs sparkling with mischief. She opened her mouth to say something else—undoubtedly something smart, but before she could expel the breath to speak, I cupped her chin, drawing her face closer, pressing a sweet, closed-mouthed kiss to her lips. I let our lips linger connected for a bit before slowly pulling back to look at Juniper once again. She was adorably pouty, eyes closed, lips still in full pucker as she let out a low groan.

"Really? Is that all you g—" she started but was quickly shut up when I captured her lips once again.

This kiss was decidedly less chaste as my

tongue took advantage of catching her off guard with her mouth open. Our tongues dueled for dominance as the kiss increased in intensity, Juniper trying desperately to take the lead, but I wasn't allowing it. My hands, which were cradling her face, moved down her body, to land at her hips, shifting her, settling her atop my lap. She murmured her approval at the shift in position, lacing her hands together behind my neck and pushing herself closer to me. I detangled our mouths, licking a trail from her ear the hollow of her throat, which caused her to throw her head back as I suckled her neck, sure to leave behind bruises as evidence of my presence on her body.

Running my tongue along her collarbone caused Juniper to let out a shuddering moan as she began a slow grind in my lap. I chuckled at her response before bringing our mouths back together in another torrid kiss, only breaking when the necessity of breathing reared its ugly head. At the conclusion of the kiss, Juniper rested her forehead on my shoulder, slumping into my embrace. We sat there for a few moments in silence, breathing falling in tandem.

"Well, shit. Now that? Is what I call a great first kiss," she quipped.

I couldn't do anything but laugh in response. We sat cocooned in silence for a few moments more until Juniper lifted her head from my shoulder and leaned in to kiss me again. She clearly hadn't had her fill as she pressed her lips against mine in slow succession, each press lingering longer than the previous contact. I captured her lower lip between my teeth sucking it into my mouth, trying to take over the kiss, but Juniper pulled back with a frown.

"What's wrong?" I asked.

"Are you a control freak? Do you always need to have the upper hand?"

"That came out of nowhere."

She shook her head, "It came from right now. I'm settled atop your lap, clearly enjoying myself, kissing you, but instead of just going with the flow, you just had to take over."

I laughed, but quickly sobered once I realized she wasn't joking at all. And my laughter deepened the crease in her forehead that appeared when she frowned.

"You're serious right now? You're in my lap, grinding on my hard dick, my hands are all over your ass, and I'm supposed to be a passive participant?"

"What happened to your caution? Moving based on my level of comfort? Letting me take the lead?"

"Are you uncomfortable right now?"

"Well, no, but..."

I shook my head, taking a moment to think about my words before speaking. I needed to clear, but inoffensive.

"Sweetheart, I'm not sure what kinda b level niggas you've been with before, but that's not how I roll. There's no power struggle here, love, just two people enjoying themselves...or at least I thought we were both enjoying ourselves. If there's something I'm doing that you don't like or that you don't want, I know you have no problem opening that pretty ass mouth and telling me, so what is this really about?"

Juniper remained silent, trying to shift off of my lap, "Maybe I should go. I should probably go."

I held her firmly in place, hands braced on her hips, "No running."

"I'm not running. I'd just like to go now."

"I'm not into holding anyone hostage, so if that's what you wish..."

I released my hold, allowing her to slide off of my lap. She stood in front of me, motionless and staring for a moment before moving back toward the apartment to gather her things. I followed right behind her, not saying anything, completely confused by what had shifted, but knowing I didn't want to say shit else that could possibly ruin the chances of seeing her again. I was no sucka ass nigga, but I also wasn't stupid. We'd reached some sort of impasse that I was sure we would work out whenever Juniper sorted out whatever was going on in her head. For now, I just followed her through the house and down the stairs, to walk her to her car.

We reached her car and I put her bag in the trunk before escorting her to the driver side door and opening it for her.

"Have a good night, sweetheart," I said, "Maybe next time we do this, I'll call you up and ask you out...you know the proper way."

We both laughed at that and I expected her to get in the car and continue on her merry little way, but Juniper turned toward me suddenly. She stared at me for a couple of seconds before speaking.

"I...had a good time tonight, Quincy."

"Me too, Juniper," I replied.

She laughed, "No for real, I did have a really good time tonight."

I grabbed her hand, moving us out of the street to rest against the passenger side of her cat.

"So, what happened? How did we go from the start of my daily fantasies for the past week to..." I waved a hand around, "Whatever this awkward shit is now?"

"You're really direct," Juniper hedged.

"I am. Lived life too long in ambiguity with too many folks. Can't operate that way and keep my sanity. Clear and direct is the only way to be 'round these parts. So, are you done sidestepping my question yet, or...?"

"Why couldn't you just go with the flow?"

"I thought we were flowing rather nicely, sweetheart."

Juniper groaned and threw her head back. I laughed instantly picking up what was going on here now. She was the control freak that she accused me of being. And because I didn't fall back and let her have her way she was frustrated. It was cute, her inability to just vocalize that.

"So, since we were flowing why couldn't you just sit back and say, 'ok sweetheart, do ya thang!'?"

"Because while you were doing your thang, my thang made it virtually impossible just to sit still, but be clear," I said, stepping in, placing an arm on either side of her and leaning down to speak directly into her ear, "If you wanna be in control like Janet, you're gonna have to tie me down. The only way I'm not taking over is if I'm literally restrained."

At the end of that statement, I delivered a lingering kiss to her neck, right below her ear before attempting to move out of her space. Juniper had different ideas though, threading her fingers behind my neck, joining our mouths in a kiss, controlling the tempo with soft nibbles and suckling my lips. My hands dropped from beside her head to her ass, sandwiching her between the car and my quickly reappearing hardness. Juniper groaned, deepening the kiss. I used the grip on her ass to lift her from the ground, bringing her legs to wrap around my waist, forgetting where we were and everything else that was not Juniper and her insistent grinding against my erection and soul-robbing kisses.

Once again, the necessity of breathing caused us to move away from each other and that separation allowed clarity to sink in and I let Juniper's legs back down to the ground. Her breathing was labored, eyes closed, lips parted as she took in breath after breath. After about ten seconds, she grabbed my hand leading me back toward my place.

"Ok, yeah. I'm definitely fucking you tonight."

JUJU

I HAD DECIDED that I was going to fuck Quincy tonight around thirty minutes after our initial misunderstanding. After I quickly got over being creeped out, I realized his intentions were good and we started vibing. He seemed like a nice guy. And that print in his grey sweats that he'd changed into after we decided to hang out and order some food sealed the deal. Honestly, it had been too long since I'd had some and I was like a cat in heat. And I dropped hints all night, which he chose to ignore until I gave him no further chances of ignoring. But then...then it all went to shit. Because I got on my Juju, ruler of all that she surveys shit, and Quincy? He definitely didn't seem like the type of man who would eventually become subservient; I was now coming to find out. Nevertheless, that didn't quell my desire to have this man embedded so deeply within my walls that I forgot where he ended, and I began. So, I got over myself, strapped my boots up, and invited myself back into his space to get what I didn't know I came for but was more than ready to receive.

After my declaration, he said nothing, just allowed me to lead him back into his place. We crossed the threshold for his apartment, but I stopped short after closing the door. I knew that his bedroom was near the back of the space because I'd seen two additional doors when I used the restroom earlier, but I wasn't sure which of the two doors led to where I wanted to go.

"Lead the way, sir," I said, all bravado on full display despite feeling...not nervous, but also very nervous.

I'd initiated sex on many occasions and in many circumstances after spending far less time with a man that Quincy and I had spent tonight, but something about this seemed...different. I couldn't put a finger on what was different or why it was, but I just felt it in my gut. And my gut had never let me down, but my gut was also not finna stop me from letting Q get in my guts, so there was also that. Instead of leading me to the bedroom, Quincy redirected our steps toward the couch in his living room.

"Are you sure about this? I want you to be sure about this because a few short minutes ago..."

I dropped my head on a groan. Because while my pussy was definitely on board, my brain wasn't one hundred percent sure.

"Can I say something without it going to a weird place?"

"It'll only get weird if you take it there," Quincy replied, smirking.

"Aight, so boom. I...this...," I started before taking a second to collect my thoughts so that I could clearly express my thoughts. The only problem was everything in my head was a jumble and I had no concise way of expressing what I was thinking.

And Quincy in an incredibly brilliant display of patience, just sat waiting for me to gather my thoughts.

"Does this feel different to you? Like...I don't know. I can't really explain it, but all of this? The random train encounter. You being the one to work on my car at Holt's? Tonight? It almost feels like it's divinely orchestrated, you know? What are the odds of us having never seen each other before as much as we've both moved around this town, but we have enough mutual followers on Instagram of all places to connect us? Well, tonight was wholly by your design, but all of those other things? Seemed...fated?" Juniper didn't wait for an answer as she continued, "I just don't want to fall into bed with you tonight and possibly ruin something that could be really special."

Quincy let out a low chuckle.

"That's silly, right? It is. I'm buggin. Which way's your bedroom?" I said, grabbing his hand to try and pull him up off the couch.

He countered by dragging me down to sit on his lap before speaking.

"It's not silly. Something about this does feel different. I don't know what it is either, but I'm glad you stopped us from making a mistake. Can't have you not respecting me after I gave you my virginity tonight," Quincy said, with a completely straight face.

"Oh my god, can you be serious? I'm for real," I said, burrowing my head into his shoulder.

His flip response should have pissed me off, but I was more embarrassed than anything. God, even my reactions to things that would have normally sent me running the other way normally were being affected by this man.

"Hey," he said softly, causing me to pull back to be able to look him in the face again.

His face bore the ghost of a smile as if he'd been trying to curtail it before he spoke.

"Yeah?"

"I was serious, you know. About this feeling different? But I'm leaning into it, trying something new. The worst that can happen is another heartbreak, but honestly? I feel it's safe with you and I know you're safe with me—so if you can get on board with that? We'll take things as they come. That sound good to you?"

I nodded once before verbally responding, "Yeah. That sounds good to me."

"All right, now that that's settled," Quincy said, tapping my thigh so I'd raise up," Let's get you outta here and home safely."

"You don't wanna..."

"Hell yeah I do, but you're not ready yet, sweetheart. You'll know when it's time. C'mon."

And with that, he led me back out of his house and into my car. I pulled off, looking in the rearview to see Quincy still standing near the curb I'd pulled away from. I tooted my horn once before making a left at the stop sign to continue on my journey home. That seemed to jolt him as he threw a hand up in salute toward my direction, then turned back to go into his house.

I sat lounging on the couch in the den listlessly

watching an SVU marathon, as per my usual Sunday routine. If no one else requested my time, I had a long-standing date with the USA network and their themed crime drama marathons. The house was quiet, so I assumed Noelle was off somewhere with Jay, which was fine by me. I could use a bit of quiet, contemplative time. I'd been burning the candle at both ends this week, weaving MYOP workshops between my current roster of web design clients.

We normally conducted the bulk of our MYOP workshops on the weekend, with the occasional Friday appointment, but for some reason, Wednesday was becoming an increasingly more popular booking day as well. Joey was talking about adding some hump day specials to capitalize on this growth, but I honestly just didn't even have the brain bandwidth to think about what all that would entail. We were growing more rapidly than anticipated and I wanted to talk to Joey about possibly bringing in a couple more facilitators to help alleviate some of the strain from our schedules. There were a couple of folks who were in class with us when we were getting our certs that I thought would be dope additions to our movement. I whipped out my phone to make a note to bring this back up when we met for lunch tomorrow.

I'd damn near fallen asleep after a few episodes when I heard my name being yelled from the front foyer. It was Noelle and she was hella turnt for some reason, so I dragged myself from reclining on the couch to see what it was she wanted.

"Hey Junie B—what is wrong with you?" Noelle asked, her brow furrowed.

"Damn, I look bad?"

"Not bad, but you definitely have a lil sour look on your face. What's going on, you good baby girl?"

"Not really," I said, surprising myself because that was definitely not what I was prepared to say in my brain.

Noelle grabbed my hand and dragged me back into the den. She shut off the TV before speaking.

"What's going on?"

"I...don't know, honestly, No. I mean...life is good right? Both of my businesses are flourishing. All of you guys are in good health and good spirits. I'm still fine as fuck, but something...just is off. I'm all off kilter and I can't call it."

"So, I didn't wanna say it, but you've been kind of...off since your whole Instagram shot shooting incident. And, sis, if your confidence is knocked because some nigga didn't respond to you hollering at him..."

"Wow, NoNo, tell me how you really feel, then."

"Nooooo," Noelle practically yelled, "I didn't mean it like that! I'm just saying. I'm used to you letting ish like this roll off. You don't even take a lot of downtime after breakups, but one rebuff has you shook?"

"First of all, there was no rebuff. I actually spent the day with him yesterday?"

Noelle gasped, raised a brow, and said, "So we holding out on each other now?"

"So was I supposed to break into brudda's last night, interrupt your post-coital glow to tell you about how I almost got piped but messed it up by being weird?"

Noelle held up a hand, "Wait. A. Minute. Back it up, gym shoe. Start from the beginning."

I ran down the circumstances to me ending up at Quincy's place and all of the rest of the night, sparing no detail because I knew that if no one else kept it funky with me, NoNo would. I finished my story with a sigh and Noelle said nothing. We sat in silence for a good two or three minutes before she had any reaction. And that reaction was to burst into a high-pitched shrieking laugh, which annoyed the hell out of me.

"Not sure anything I said was funny but go off."

"Awwwww Junie, don't be that way," Noelle said, reaching out to embrace me.

I deftly avoided her outstretched arms and rolled my eyes.

"Just...forget it. Nevermind. What had you so crunk when you stepped in?"

"Nah-uh baby girl. Don't even think about shutting down. You know what the problem is right?"

"No. I don't. You do?!"

"Yeah, baby. You like him."

"That's no secret, No. I said he was a cool dude and we had a good time," I replied, exasperated.

"Noooo, baby. You like him. And you're freaking out because you think it's strange or too soon or you're in denial of your feelings for him. But maybe that IG caption wasn't just in jest. He makes you feel something. And I ain't talking about in ya loins, I'm talking about that man moving your foundation and you're fucked up behind it because you've never felt this way. Dassit!" Noelle said and spread her hands in a ta-da fashion.

"I...you...shit. Shit! Is that...shit!"

I sank down into the couch groaning.

"That's a good thing, Junie B. Buck up," Noelle

said, waving her hands in my face, "Liking someone has its perks."

She kept moving her hands wildly and finally the light caught onto and almost blinded me with its misdirection of sunrays but caused me to focus on its cause. I grabbed Noelle's hand and screamed. The gorgeous ring that Jay had shown me just a few short days ago now sat beautifully perched on the fourth finger of her left hand. I marveled over how beautifully the delicately filigreed band rested upon Noelle's slender finger.

"Oh my god you have to tell me everything. Forget about my mess! How'd he do it? When'd he do it? I can't believe he did it without telling me!"

"You knew this was happening?"

"Sis, please. Everybody and our mama knew it was inevitable. Nobody knew when though. Shout out to Jay," I said, sarcastically.

"You wanna hear how it went down or nah?"

"Yes, please, now!"

"All right so it's not really a glamorous story. We were supposed to go out with last night with TJ and his wife, but one of their fifty kids got sick or something, idk, but it resulted in us just bumming around the house. Like…it was bad. My hair wasn't combed. I was in a ratty pair of his old basketball shorts and one of his old t-shirts. Jay had been kinda…skittish all day, but I knew that he was pre-occupied with some recent bs with Dude, Where's My Bar? So, I figured his behavior had to do with that. Anyway, that's not important to the story. So, we're sitting in the basement, watching Russ n'em getting whooped and Jay's like "do you need the ice in your drink refreshed?" And I looked over to give him the boy what look, and he was sitting there with the ring box opened and a stupid ass grin on his face."

"Oh my God he's so corny and in the best of ways!" I gushed, "Then what happened?"

"He got down on one knee, said a lot of really beautiful things that my brain still hasn't fully processed and asked me to be his wife. And the rest was history."

I sighed, damn near swooning out of my socks because that proposal was so Jay and NoNo. Low key, corny, no theatrics and filled with love. And for a moment, in the midst of my happiness, I felt a little put out. Now that Jay had finally popped the question? The Cheese stands alone. I was now the only unpartnered Holliday sister.

"Uh oh, what's that look?" Noelle asked.

I brushed her off, not wanting my silly thoughts to mar what was supposed to be a happy moment. I'd work through my mess later. Now was the time to bask in my big sister's glow.

"It's nothing. I'm happy for you, No. And for Jay, too. Y'all finally got it right!"

"Excuse you?" Noelle scoffed.

"I said what I said."

"But back to you, chica. Don't think you're slick! Honestly, how are you feeling about this guy... what's his name again?"

"Quincy."

"How do you feel about Quincy?"

"Honestly? Like I want to see him right now."

"Yeah?"

"Yeah. Is that weird?"

"Does it feel weird?"

"Kinda?"

"You don't sound sure, Junie B."

"I don't know," I whined sounding all of eight years old.

"You know you sound like Jordie right now, right?"

"Can you just tell me what to do? Please," I begged which did nothing but garner another one of those infuriating peals of laughter from Noelle.

"Do what makes you feel good, boo. That's the only advice I got. Stop fighting it and lean into the good."

"But I don't know if it makes me feel good?"

"Trust me, sis, it does make you feel good. You're just trying so hard to fight the feelings because they're foreign. But that googly-eyed twinkle in your eye from just simply saying his name? That lets me know everything I need to know about you and him and y'all."

"Which is?"

Noelle just laughed again, shaking her head.

"Call him and find out."

"HELLO?"

"Wow, he finally answers!" a peeved feminine voice crowed through my phone.

"Here we go..."

"Hey, daddy!"

"Hey, baby girl."

"It's so good to hear your voice. So glad you're alive over there. You sound well."

"And you sound as dramatic as your mother."

At her offended gasp, I chuckled. Babygirl was being dramatic though. I hadn't talked to her in maybe a couple of weeks and she was acting like it had been months. I called myself giving her and Charity the space to enjoy their annual mother-daughter bonding trip to whatever island they went this year. I'd expected her to call me as soon as they'd touched back down in the states, but Quincey Junior and I had been playing the longest game of phone tag known to mankind.

"Woooooow, somebody gets a lil girlfriend and now he's feeling himself," Junie laughed, "It be ya own daddies out here."

"Tread lightly, little girl," I warned with a laugh.

Juniper and I had fallen into a groove after our initial bumpy starts. We were in constant contact, making time to see each other when our schedules permitted, but also not super pressed when they didn't. In the few weeks that we'd been kicking it, I'd only seen her in person maybe four or five times, the last one I had to damn near threaten her to accept my invitation to take a break. She recently landed a job that involved a complete web presence overhaul for a chain of cupcake shops that were cropping up in our area and it had her working around the clock.

Instead of working from home like she normally did, she was using the shared workspace that she and Joey rented for MYOP. I insisted that she at least take a break to eat before she ran herself completely ragged, which led to our first argument. She accused me of overstepping and I accused her of overreacting. It was a whole mess, hence why I was on my way to make it up to her now. A quick stop at the nursery to pick her up a nice, leafy green plant as a means of apology was stop one of my apology world tour.

It was strange because any other woman I would have written off as being melodramatic and not worth the antics, but something about Juniper had me hooked. I couldn't quite put my finger on it, but she had better get used to me being around because I didn't plan on going anywhere for quite a while, if at all.

"Daddy, are you listening?" Junie yelled.

"Sure am, baby girl."

"You're a terrible liar, Senior. Now that you're

actually listening, I asked when will I get to meet my new stepmommy?"

"You know you gotta chill on calling her that before you slip up in front of her?"

"Well how am I supposed to slip up if you never even introduce us?"

"Quincey, please."

She giggled at the exasperation in my tone. She knew she was working my nerves and delighted in the shit. I swear Ant was right, I really did need to enact some boundaries with this little girl, but I guess I might be about fifteen years too late on getting her to respect the enforcement of these boundaries.

"I'm on my way to see Juniper now. She's been really busy the past few weeks, but I'll see what we can work out so y'all can finally meet."

"This sounds like a lie, but okay, daddy."

"Did you call to get on my nerves or did this call have a purpose?" I asked, clearly annoyed now.

"Somebody's testy. I really was calling to check in since we hadn't had any daddy-daughter time in a minute. I miss you, old man."

"Sounds like your pockets are getting light..."

"Nooooo, for real daddy! I'm coming over this weekend, okay? We need to catch up on Walking Dead anyway...unless you're watching it with your little girlfriend."

"Quincey," I said, my voice holding a note of censure.

"Okay! Sorry, dad! I really was just joking. And I was serious about wanting to meet her soon, too."

"I hear you baby girl and I was serious about asking her if she was ready for all of that?"

"All of that?"

"You heard me."

I had finally made it to the nursery and didn't want to have to juggle being on the phone with trying to get some assistance from the people inside, so I rang off with Quincey after confirming that I would be picking her up on Friday as soon as she was done with drill team practice. I must've looked like a fish out of the water as soon as I walked into the nursery a woman approached, enthusiastically offering to help me out. That enthusiasm waned slightly after I told her I was looking for a plant for my girl, but she did end up helping me find something perfect.

The first time I went to the MYOP office space, I noticed that every bit of free space in their office was covered with greenery and I later found out that it was Juniper's doing. She'd read some article about the benefits of plants in office environments and, in Jonique's choice of words, "went OD on the plant shit." The result was a lushly decorated space with a Zen aura. I paid for the plant, with a promise to also leave a review on Google or Yelp and made my way to Juniper. I didn't call to let her know I was coming, a big risk since I was sure she was still pissed at me, but I also didn't want her to have an out and leave the joint before I had a chance to pop up.

When I arrived at the workspace, I could see Juniper through the window, looking fine and stressed as hell at the same damn time. She ran a hand through her hair before bringing her forehead to rest in her palm. The slight up and down movements of her shoulders let me know that she was either employing a deep breathing exercise or Bankhead bouncing. I tapped on the window, lightly, to get her attention so that she could unlock the exterior door and allow my entry. The noise made her jump slightly before her gaze focused on me grinning like a fool with a plant in one hand and a poke bowl from her favorite spot in the other. Stop two on my apology world tour was to Hoke Poke, her newest obsession.

Juniper grinned in spite of herself, rolled her eyes and came to let me in.

"You still mad?"

"Dogs go mad, people get angry," she countered, words laced with warmth letting me know she definitely wasn't that upset.

"Okay then," I nodded, moving across the threshold and right into her space, "Are you still angry?"

"When was I angry?" she replied with a grin before turning and walking back into the MYOP workspace.

I followed behind her, settling the plant in an empty space right in the middle of the large window that took up a quarter of the front of the room before walking over to her desk where she sat perched upon the edge. I nudged her knees apart, standing in the gap before lowering to speak directly in her ear.

"So I'm not still an... What was it you called me? An overstepping boar who needs to mind his own God-given business, I believe it was?"

She tilted her head to the side, bringing her left hand to rest upon her chin.

"Hmmm, I don't recall."

I chuckled, placing a soft kiss right beneath her ear before trailing over to her mouth for a proper greeting kiss. Her body formed to mine immediately, legs tightening around me as she pulled me closer to get her fill. When we finally separated, her eyes remained closed for a second and the ghost of a dreamy smile graced her lips. After a few seconds, she opened her eyes, a smile on full blast.

"I owe you an apology."

I reared back, surprised, "Oh word?"

Juniper nodded, "Yeah, I was on one the other day. And Joey let me have it as soon as you left that day. I'd actually planned on surprising you today—the first day I've had any room to breathe—but you beat me to it."

"You're all good, sweetheart."

She shook her head, "Nah, I was out of line. And acting like a petulant child because I was over-whelmed. And instead of just letting you do what you were trying to do and take care of me, I went off the deep end because...Quincy..."

I held up a hand to stop her, "We're yet working on you. No further explanation needed."

She rolled her eyes, laughing, "See, here you go being perfect."

"Far from perfect, sweetheart, but definitely pa-tient. Hell, I wouldn't be able to handle Junie if I wasn't patient."

"Whaaaaat? You just called me Junie? You never call me anything but Juniper, despite my asking you several times to not."

"Nah, I wasn't referring to you as Junie, babe. I was talking about Junior...speaking of her...she asked to meet you today."

Juniper stiffened in my arms and attempted to put some space between us, but I wasn't letting that happen. I tightened my hold around her waist with one hand and used the other to tip her head up so that our eyes were meeting. She looked skittish as if she was ready to cut and run for the nearest exit.

"Relax," I said, "I told her I'd run it by you before we made any solid plans."

Juniper and I had talked about Quincey Junior in the abstract—she knew that I had a teenage daughter, I'd shared funny stories or mentioned her when something in our conversations reminded me of her, but we'd never actually talked about the two of them meeting. I knew I needed to tread lightly with Juniper, as she was barely cemented by the fact that this thing between us wouldn't dissipate and disappear before she knew it. Bringing the kid into the mix before we'd gotten on solid ground would be a recipe for disaster.

"I think...I think that would be nice. To finally meet her. I feel like I know her a bit after you've shared so much about her with me."

"Oh perfect, she'll be over this weekend, you can come over Friday and kick it with us."

Juniper's eyes widened to comically large proportions before I let my laughter go and assured her that I wasn't trying to bring them together that soon. I'd give her a couple of weeks to get herself together and then we'd figure things out from there. I wasn't in a rush to make it happen because I knew once it happened I'd become the minority in my damn home and I wasn't ready to deal with any of that quite yet. Nicknames aside, my Junie and Juniper had way too much in common from their smart mouths to an inexplicable obsession with every single show in that love and hip-hop franchise. Once those two teamed up, it would be a wrap for my sanity.

"You play too much," Juniper said, swatting me on the ass.

"Aight, I gotta get outta here. Prent needs me to close up tonight, so I'm going in for a few hours. I'll call you later though."

"Actually, you mind if I come by tonight?" Juniper asked, "I put together a little something for you...you know, for my apology?"

"Now this, I have to see. Yeah, I should be done at the garage around nine thirty, is that too late?"

"Nope, I'll be at your place by ten."

"Aight babe," I said, leaning down to give her one last kiss before I headed into work, "See you then."

I was almost out of the office when Juniper called out to me.

"Q! The plant?"

"Instructions on caretaking in the bag with your lunch."

"You really do think of everything," she said, more to herself than to me, so I just grinned as I strolled on out the door without a reply.

━━

I was laid out on the couch, damn near asleep when the loud buzzing of my phone jarred me awake. I grabbed it with one hand while swiping the other down my face. I came home after work, took a quick shower and sat down to watch a lil SportsCenter while waiting for Juniper to arrive and slid into the quickest nod. The phone buzzed again, alerting me to two new text messages.

On the way. You still up? – Juniper

Sorry for the delay, unexpected stop for supplies.
:) - Juniper

I replied that I was awake, and the door was open, curious about what sort of supplies this whole apology situation she had put together required. Then I actually unlocked the door downstairs and my apartment door, so she could just come right on in. Settling back on the couch, I gave my attention back to SportsCenter until she arrived. Actually staying awake, however, wasn't in the plans as I dozed once again.

I was awakened from my slumber by Juniper softly calling my name as she trailed her fingers all over my face, playing in my beard and booping my nose until I opened my eyes. I cracked them to see her leaning over me, grinning.

"Wake up, sleepyhead," she whispered briefly nuzzling my neck before walking away, "I worked really hard on this apology and I'll lose my nerve if I have to wait 'til morning to do it."

I sat up, yawning and stretching, running a hand through my locs before focusing my attention on where Juniper stood blocking the television. When my eyes finally focused on her form, they almost bugged out of my head.

"Goddamn."

She was wearing some sort of...hell, I don't know what material this catsuit was made of, just that it molded to all her curves perfectly accentuating her high, perky breasts, shapely hips and all that ass. Her hair was splayed about her face, in wild waves cascading past her shoulders. She busied herself with turning off the television and connecting her phone to my Bluetooth soundbar before making her way back over to me. She pulled me up from the couch to sit in one of the armless chairs flanking the sofa.

"Can you behave, or will you need to be restrained?" she asked as she stood in front of me looking like a fantasy that was illegal in at least twenty-four of the forty-eight contiguous states.

My answer was nonverbal as I reached out to grab her, which she quickly sidestepped.

"Restraints it is," she said, sauntering over to a bag she had placed on the floor near the television. She walked back over to me holding what appeared to be a red velvet rope and suddenly the music playing in the background clicked for me.

"Yoooooo, no you didn't."

Juniper didn't respond, just smirked as she swaggered back over to me and tied my hands behind my back.

During one of our marathon phone conversations, I told her that my sexual awakening as a very young teen came via Janet Jackson. One of my older cousins was a huge fan and was convinced that she was going to go on and dance for Janet. So, the entire summer that she was supposed to be babysitting me, she spent hella time watching and re-watching The Velvet Rope Live DVD trying in vain to teach herself the choreography so that when Janet called she'd be ready to go at the drop of a dime. Never mind the fact that we were in the middle of the country with no connections to any of the famous legion of choreographers that Janet employed to seek out new talent.

As annoyed as I got with Tika for her incessant watching of that damn DVD, I was front and center for two segments. The first was when Janet performed "I Get Lonely" and ripped that button down open to showcase her fantastic rack, but the second and most important was when Janet performed a cut off the cd that was called "Rope Burn". Janet was famous for bringing a nigga on stage and tying him down and torturing him to the sweetest death using sensual choreography and blatant sexuality to drive them insane. There were many nights that I fell asleep or woke up to a dream of being the dude that Janet tied down on stage. I shared this with Juniper in one of our earliest conversations, but she was clearly playing attention as not "Rope Burn", but one of Janet's other baby-making tunes was piped through the speakers in my living room. As Janet sang about touching, teasing, licking and pleasing her man into submission, Juniper drove me insane with a combination of sensuality and blatant freak nasty that had me panting by the time the song ended.

"You accept my apology?" she asked, as the song ended, and Janet lamented about not being able to cum on the record before her producers faded the music out.

Once again, instead of using my words, I broke the flimsy restraint and, using both of my hands maintained a firm grip on Juniper's ass as I moved us from the living room to my bedroom in a flash. She yelped as I none too gently set her on the bed before covering her entire body with mine, hovering close, but not yet connecting our mouths. My tongue swiped her lower lip once, twice, before she grabbed my head with both her hands trying to deepen the contact. I swerved, landing a trail of kisses on her neck instead—fleeting teasing passes of my lips against her skin. Juniper groaned in discontent.

"You had your fun, now let me have mine," I said, before suckling the hollow at the base of her throat.

"You gonna keep teasing me, or you gonna have your fun?" Juniper whimpered as I slowly unzipped her little outfit, placing kisses on each inch of exposed skin.

As I peeled the fabric down her body, revealing a perfect body clad in red lace, I groaned, damn near feeling like this was going to be over before I really got started. She really pulled no punches with this apology thing, with everything down to the tiniest detail curated to appeal to what turned me on. I took a quick moment to gather my wits, shed my ball shorts, and grab a condom from my bedside table before turning my attention back to Juniper.

She'd shifted position, no longer lying down, but braced against my headboard—lower lip pulled between her teeth as she anxiously watched my every movement. I reached out, grabbing one of her delicate ankles to drag her back down toward me at the end of the bed. The movement was so swift it caught her off guard, causing her to emit a yelp as our bodies once again were flush with one another and I captured her mouth in a searing kiss. Our tongues parried before I dragged my mouth further south, my hands already busy ridding Juniper of that pesky bra, which at this point was nothing more than a barrier blocking me from fully enjoying the lush playground that was Juniper's body.

As I undid the front closure and parted the cups, I noticed that not only did Juniper have absolutely, mouthwateringly perfect breasts, but both were pierced with rose gold colored, thin, barely visible hoops. I looked up to catch her eye like "are you serious" and she just smirked, which soon turned into an open-mouthed whine as I traced her areolas with the tip of my tongue.

"Sssssssss," she hissed, a shuddering breath wracking her body as I went back and forth between gliding my tongue along her sensitive flesh and nibbling before sucking one of her nipples into my mouth, biting down gently while pinching the other.

Juniper was vocal, loudly proclaiming her approval as my mouth charted a course down her body, leaving her breasts to settle between her legs with a deep inhale before removing her panties and diving in face first. She smelled like heaven and tasted like ecstasy as I lost myself in her, delighting in the sounds she made as I used my mouth and fingers to create a delightfully wonderful mess between her legs. In what seemed like no time, her thighs were shaking and she was dripping wet as she reached a climax. I locked my arms around the lower half of her body, locking her in place as I continued to feast upon the treasure between her legs. Her back bowed from the bed as she shrieked out something that was unintelligible gibberish.

"Quinceeeeeeee. Please," Juniper whined, rapping the top of my head, trying her best to get me to ease up.

I licked her one final time, very slowly while my tongue lingered on her clit, teasing a little longer before making my way back up to look her in the face. Her eyes fluttered open, a dreamy smile covering her face before she reached up and pulled my face down for a gentle, sex-laced kiss that soon turned into a blazing inferno of desire. She kept nudging at my shoulder and I finally acquiesced, rolling over on my back and bringing Juniper to rest atop me.

"You just gotta be in control, huh Lil Janet?" I joked.

Her head dropped as she laughed, then reached over to the side table to grab the condom. At the ripping of that packet, we were back at it again. She quickly sheathed me and slid down slowly, coming down halfway before slowly ascending once again. She repeated her teasing strokes until I finally pulled her onto me completely. Fully seated, she began to move in slow, winding circles, encouraged by my hands rhythmically squeezing her ass in conjunction with her motions.

I shifted, sitting up to settle my attention back on her breasts and those unexpected nipple rings. Juniper moaned as I rolled her nipples between my thumb and forefinger before alternating between pinching and squeezing. Her slow winding circles shifted to a quick up and down bounce, her ass jiggling against my thighs with each downward stroke. Grabbing her hips, I stroked up to meet her bounces and soon that tell-tale tremble in her thighs that signaled a climax began again. Moments later, Juniper collapsed into me, whimpering through her climax and milking me into one of my own. After taking a few moments to allow Juniper to come down, I moved her hair aside, making sure to speak directly into her ear as she seemed to drift asleep.

"Apology accepted."

JUJU

I WAS JARRED outta my sleep by two things, the smell of bacon and a velvety smooth voice singing along to "You Are the Best Thing" by Ray LaMontagne. I rolled over into my pillow trying to muffle the sound and get back into REM when the events of the previous night came flooding back to me. I peeled my eyes open to see a room that I had no cause to pay much attention to last night, but couldn't soak in enough of the details this morning. The room was anchored by the large, charcoal grey colored sleigh bed, with a tufted headboard in which I found myself snuggled currently. Linens and window dressings were in various shades of grey, but the monochromatic look managed to give an aura of warmth and depth instead of being static and flat. I went to run my fingers through my hair and found it to be a matted, tangled mess. Sighing, I tried to quickly hop out of bed to investigate just how crazy it looked in the en-suite bathroom's mirror, but the sound of the music I heard getting louder made me freeze in my tracks.

"Fuck it. He'll get what he gets," I muttered,

vainly trying to shake my hair to attain some sem-
blance of cute.

Quincy entered the room, balancing a few
plates on his arms, looking like a damn work of art—
sculpted biceps, a sixty-four pack, and, my weak-
ness, those damn v-cuts, dips, whatever they were
called. Meanwhile, I looked like I was about to say
"ohhhhhtay", hair on straight Buckwheat status. He
walked over and placed the plates on the nightstand
on my side of the bed before holding up a finger and
running out of the room again. When he returned,
he placed the glasses of apple juice and the bottle of
ketchup that he was holding on the nightstand and
leaned down to give me a kiss. What I'm sure he
meant to be a quick brush of the mouth turned into
my hands twining themselves behind his neck and
drawing him down to the bed and into a deeper
kiss.

Pulling back slowly, Quincy said, "Now that's
what I call a good morning greeting. Fuck this
food!"

Then proceeded to nibble his way down my
neck when my stomach sounded off like a lion in
the wild. Quincy immediately busted out laughing
as I lowered my head in embarrassment and
groaned. He nudged me to move closer to the
middle of the bed before settling in and passing me
a plate and a glass of juice. Quincy had made us
each a simple breakfast sandwich with eggs, cheese,
and hand-pressed sausage patties on a biscuit and a
side of hash browns.

"You're good with eating in your bed?"

"Are you a toddler? Besides, after all the nasty
things you did to me last night? These sheets need
to get changed anyway."

I fake gasped, collapsing into laughter, "Me? I have no idea what you're talking about."

"Mmmmhmmm, sure, whatever you say."

"Hey..."

"Is for horses."

I rolled my eyes before continuing, "Were you listening to Ray LaMontagne earlier?"

"Girl, what you know about Ray?"

"Nah, what do you know about Ray? Wouldn't have pegged you for a fan."

Quincy scoffed, fake offended, "Excuse you? Is that some stereotyping I'm hearing right now? I'll have you know I contain multitudes, thank you very much."

I held up my hands, laughing, "My bad, Mr. Finley, didn't mean to offend."

"It ain't all rappity rap over here."

I laughed, "No, but for real...my real point was you sounded good. I didn't know you could sing."

"Never came up. But yeah, I can do a lil somethin'..." Quincy replied, reaching for my plate and glass to place them back on the side table next to the bed.

I relaxed a bit further, sinking down into his pillows, "You take requests?"

"Girl it's only you, have it your way, and if you want you can decide..." Quincy sang right into my ear as he slid closer to me, wrapping me up in an embrace.

I shuddered upon hearing the opening line to D'Angelo's "Untitled" a song that I wore out multiple cd copies of Voodoo listening to over and over and over again on the hand-me-down radio that Noelle left behind when she went to college. Q knew exactly what he was doing as he trailed his lips from my ear to my neck, pressing soft, suckling kisses along my collarbone. I shuddered as he darted his tongue darted out to trail along the same path he'd previously kissed. He looked up with a smirk and I knew I needed to curtail this before I lost more day than I already had.

"As much as I'd like to continue this..." I started.

Quincy just continued about his business as if I hadn't spoken at all, dragging the covers down to expose my body, eyes hungrily taking all of me in before he resumed those spine-tingling kisses, trailing from my neck to my breasts. Quincy blew out a soft stream of air, and my nipples immediately hardened, as if they were standing at the ready for his attention and he spared no time giving them what they sought. His tongue laved my skin, nipping and suckling until he had me squirming, damn near climax. I moaned as he dragged his right hand from resting on my hip to play between my legs, thumb immediately zeroing in on my clit as he pressed down and rotated twice. My legs opened of their own volition as if that were some sort of magic combination. His long, thick, skilled fingers deftly moved to part my lips, playing in the wetness that started as soon as his mouth connected with my skin. In next to no time I felt myself ascending, moans growing louder and cusses aplenty flowing from my mouth as he drove my body to the brink of ecstasy. As I came down from my orgasm, my eyes alighted on the clock and I groaned in frustration.

"Let me guess, you gotta get up outta here," Quincy said.

"Unfortunately."

"Mmmhmm, I see how it is. Come over here in

the dead of night, take advantage of me, then take off."

"Shut up! It is not like that!"

"Yeah yeah, say anything to avoid bruising my ego," Quincy said, peering up from where he was still splayed between my legs with an amused grin on his handsome face.

He pressed a kiss to my left inner thigh, then the right before pulling himself up and letting me up to get my things so I could get my life together before heading into the office. I had the final meeting with my web design clients this morning during which I'd present the final website and barring any major changes, I'd be able to implement and hang this project up for good, which would free up a lot of my time. I ran out to the living room to grab my bag, took a quick shower, and dressed before promising Quincy that I'd see him a little later for lunch.

___

"Ooh, now I'll never get over you until I find somethin' new, that gets me high like you do," I sang along with Ella Mai.

My meeting with Cupcakin' went off without a hitch. They loved all of the responsive design features that I added to the site that made the user experience friendlier. The current iteration of their website was clunky, filled with terrible flash animation and an autoplay MIDI version of Rihanna's "Birthday Cake". I was horrified when I first viewed it because it looked like it was built on Geocities and how in the hell they found a MIDI version of that song was something I didn't even care to figure out. Nevertheless, I brought them into the 21st Century and they were beyond pleased, as evidenced in the lil somethin' somethin' extra that appeared on the check the owner Cierra slid my way at the close of our appointment.

Instead of heading home, I stayed in the MYOP workspace, reviewing some of the applications submitted by folks who responded to our postings on indeed.com. The folks I had in mind that we'd studied with were employed and not interested in taking a chance on a startup, so we went out to the wild. The ad had only been up a few days, but we'd gotten more than a few bites. Unfortunately, many of them were going straight to the sludge pile because they weren't qualified. So here I was, singing along to "Boo'd Up" and scrolling these resumes and applicant profiles.

"Somebody's in a good mood," Joey said, as she walked in, "I guess good dick'll do that to ya. You know I want all the nasty, dirty details and don't you leave nothin' out."

"Well hello to you too, Jonique," I replied, laughing.

"Yeah yeah heffa, pleasantries! So...how'd it go down?"

Joey was my right-hand man and helped me plan my apology to Q last night, right on down to the nitty-gritty details so I shouldn't have been surprised that she wanted to know everything. The problem was, I didn't exactly feel like she needed to know everything.

"I mean, we had a good time. He accepted my apology..."

"Are you really out here tryna be coy like...wait,

awwwwww" Joey squealed, running over to hug me.

I shrugged her off, "What?"

"You like him, don't you?" she asked, grinning like a damn loon.

"Of course I like him, you know this already. We've discussed."

"Nah, heffa. You like him like him. That's why you're being cagey with the details. Normally you have no problems telling me about any of your other sexcapades, but the last guy that had you mum like this...erm, nevermind. Forget I even brought that up," Joey finished up quickly.

I closed my eyes and pushed out a sigh because I'd been waiting for her to bring him up. I thought for sure she would have brought him up after I freaked out on Quincy the first time. Or when I went through round one of my hoe phase nine months ago...or round two, three months ago, but Joey had been biding her time. We never said his name. It was the one promise I made her make if ever we were to discuss him again. He was only to be referred to as one of the male pronouns or "the only nigga to ever break my heart".

"So...okay, Joey do you really think how I'm acting similar to how things started with B—"

"Nope, you can't say his name," Joey interrupted, "Your rules, don't forget. And no, I think there are some similarities, but this definitely doesn't feel the same as that was. For one, Quincy seems way more into you than you're into him unlike with that other raggedy mother—you know what, nope. Nah, sis. We aren't going there today. I want you to give Quincy a fair shot. You can't be so concerned with protecting your heart that you never give anyone else the chance to win it. Don't let that raggedy nigga's legacy mar what your future could be with Quincy. It's unfair not only to him, but to you too, Ju."

"I know...I know. Just...easier said than done, you know?"

"I know, boo, but you gotta actively work at it, right? It's like the plants, man. Remember the first set of 'em that you brought in here? They were browning within three days. But a bit of patience and understanding and knowledge and you became a regular old green thumb outchea. Gotta apply that same energy toward this thing with Quincy, too."

"Okay, this is getting a little too Iyanla up in here now," I said, laughing trying to lighten the mood.

"Bitch please, Rhonda wish she had the sagacity that I possess, okay?!"

"You're a mess, Joey."

"Your favorite mess and you're deflecting. It's okay. I'll let you slide this time, but I just want you to be content, sis. That's all."

"I am happy!" I balked.

"I said nothing about happiness, but contentment. Happiness is fleeting, my love, a buzz, a high feeling for a moment. Contentment settles in deep down in your soul and is everlasting, unmovable. That's what I wish for you. And that's what I think Quincy can provide to and for you."

"You don't even know him, how are you so sure?"

"Have I ever been wrong before?" Joey asked, arrogance lacing her tone.

I took a second to think about it and Jonique did have an excellent judge of character and most often, her impression of a person ended up being spot on in regard to their character over time. So she may have had a point.

"Meh, I guess."

"You guess? Tuh. Know me!"

My phone began to ring before I could answer Joey's boasts. I looked down to see Quincy's name splayed across the screen and couldn't contain the smile that spread across my face instantly.

"Mmmmmhmmm, that must be Mr. Contentment now."

I said nothing to Joey, just swiped my screen to answer the call.

"Hey you," I said.

Quincy's voice sounded on edge and I was immediately on high alert. He was calling to cancel our lunch date since his daughter had been involved in a car accident. She and some friends thought they would take an off-campus lunch diversion and ended up in a fender-bender that left a few of them quite injured. Quincey Junior's mother was out of town, so my Quincy was on his way to the hospital to see about his girl. All he knew so far was that she had a broken arm and she was pretty shaken up by the accident. I let him know that I was more than fine with him having to break our plans and for him to keep me updated on Junior's progress.

———

"You know I hate the mall, why are we at the mall?" I asked Lolo.

She called me this morning talking about she wanted me to come on a ride with her and I certainly did not think that it would end up in us pulling up to the Yorktown Shopping Center. I actively avoided this place although it was a mainstay in my tween and teen years. It looked nothing like it had in those days, however, with the proliferation of restaurants and specialty shops decorating what used to be a vast parking lot.

"We're at the mall because the baby wants a Cinnabon."

"Not a cinnamon roll, but a Cinnabon in particular, huh? The baby is big on the brands already?"

"She wants what she wants, what can I say?"

"Lo," I said, "You're like twenty minutes pregnant. You don't know what's cooking in that oven quite yet."

"Whatever, it's a girl. I know it. There hasn't been a Holliday son in forever."

"Could be a Mora man in there tho," I replied, laughing.

"Ugh," Lolo grunted, "You and your brother-in-law can stop crushing my dreams out here. He swears I'm carrying Frankie Junior."

Lolo parked the car and we walked into the mall on a side entrance near the airport. She was insistent that we sit in the food court, so she could enjoy her bun fresh since as soon as we were walking up the kid behind the counter was pulling a fresh batch out of the oven. As we sat in the food court, talking and eating I kept feeling like somebody was watching me. I looked around and didn't notice anyone, in particular, paying too close attention to me but still couldn't shake that feeling. After we finished eating our Cinnabons, Lo insisted that we walk around a bit to work off the calories ingested. I suspected, however, she just wanted to do some baby shopping as she immediately nudged me in the direction of the baby store as we left the food court. Before we had taken more than a couple of steps, I heard an "excuse me!" from behind us.

I looked back to see a couple of teenaged girls heading in our direction. They were whispering and giggling to one another until they stood right in front of us.

"Your name is Juju, right?" the shorter of the two girls said.

The kid looked familiar for some reason, but I couldn't place it. She was a cute lil chocolate thing, big expressive eyes and deep-set dimples and gorgeously styled sisterlocks. Her friend was equally adorable, just a little bit taller with sepia colored skin, striking red hair, and piercing green eyes.

"Yep, that's me."

"So, I know this is like awkward or whatever because we were supposed to meet all formally, but I just saw you and figured I would just come and introduce myself now. I mean, I don't need my daddy to speak for me when you're just right here, you know? I recognized you from the IG post. And I told my cousin Sheena this was you and she said we should just come over and speak. So...hi."

As soon as she said the word daddy it occurred to me who this was standing in front of me. It was Quincey Junior. And she was right this was awkward. I didn't know what I should do, so I smiled and held out a hand for a shake. She grabbed my hand, squeezing it pretty firmly while pumping it up and down.

"Hi, it's nice to meet you, Quincey."

"Oh, you can call me Junie. That's what everybody calls me. Is that your sister?" she asked, pointing in Lolo's direction, "Dag, she's so pretty too. I told daddy that he needed to slide in your DMs before somebody else came at you because you're so fine. Like for real. You're really pretty," she prattled on, barely taking a moment to breathe.

"I thought y'all were making a run to Auntie Annie's for frozen lemonade," a deep voice rumbled.

I looked up to see a man with the same sepia colored skin as Junie's friend.

"We were Uncle Ant, but then we saw daddy's girlfriend and I came to introduce myself," Quincey Junior said.

"Uhhhh," the man I now knew to be Ant, Quincy's best friend said, "Junebug, I thought your dad was going to...ahhhh, hey, it's nice to meet you, officially Juniper. Heard a lot about you."

"Likewise," I said, "My...um...my sister and I actually are on a bit of a time crunch, but it was nice meeting you guys. Next time we'll be able to chat a little longer, yeah? All right y'all have a good day," I said quickly, grabbing Lolo at the elbow and dragging her toward the baby store that we were originally heading to.

"What in the world just happened there?" Valora asked, amusement tingeing her tone.

"I think I just got ambushed," I groaned.

I'D JUST FINISHED up an oil change when my phone rang.

"What up, Ant?"

"Bruh, remember when I told you needed to set some boundaries with Junebug?" he said in lieu of a greeting and launched into a story that had my chest getting tight as soon as he finished.

Ah shit, here we go! I thought. Apparently my too nosy for her own good daughter decided that I was taking too long and ran up on Juniper and her sister in the mall. The girls and Ant were in the mall picking up a gift for Nina's birthday and somehow got separated. All it took was a few minutes and a happy coincidence for the kid to have possibly set some bullshit in motion. I only had about half an hour left before I was supposed to be getting off and going to chill with Juniper, but I went and asked Prent to let me cut out a lil early. He gave me a lil bit of shit before telling me to get my rusty ass on outta his face. I made a quick pit stop home to shower and change my clothes and shot Juniper a text to let her know I'd be over a little earlier than we'd planned. She replied that was cool and she should be back at home by the time I arrived at her place.

Juniper and I wound up pulling up at the same time. I braced myself for...something when I got out of my car to greet her, but she said nothing beyond, "Hey you." I pulled her in for a hug, pressing a quick kiss to her lips before following her up the pathway and porch into the house.

"You want some wine?" she said, walking toward the kitchen not waiting for an answer.

I trailed behind her, crossing the threshold of the kitchen as she pulled two large glasses and a corkscrew from the minibar cart near the refrigerator. I sat down at the breakfast bar where there was a bottle of wine waiting. Juniper walked back over to where I was sitting, set the glasses down, uncorked the wine and poured herself a glass before walking out the kitchen and into the den. I grabbed the bottle of wine and my glass, following her. I sat down next to her on the couch and she immediately snuggled into my side, sighing. We sat there for a few moments in silence as she sipped her wine.

"Heard you had an interesting encounter today?" I said, finally breaking the silence.

"Yeah..."

"And how do you feel about that encounter?"

"It's fine, Q. I'm not freaking out."

"I didn't say you were. I just asked a simple—" Juniper cut me off.

"Yo, chill. I'm good. We're good. I was a little taken aback because she caught me off guard, but it's fine, baby. It was gonna happen one of these days, right?"

"Yeah, but on your terms. Not at my child's re-fusal to mind her damn business," I laughed.

"Baby. It's fine," Juniper said, leaning up to give me a kiss, "For real, I'm good."

"All right."

We sat in silence again. So many questions were running through my brain but knowing that if I pressed we'd end up in a not so good place, so I was content to sit here with my girl in my arms, sip-ping her wine with a smile on her face. Wild how this all played out, how she snuck up on me outta nowhere and now I wasn't sure how much my life had been missing until she appeared in it. I was ful-filled by my job, had more than two hands full fa-thering Junie, but Juniper's presence brought that lil somethin' somethin' extra. I chuckled a bit, shaking my head, thinking about how a damn social media app, of all things, brought us together. I imag-ined our lives together, and one day having to tell our children or grandchildren how we met.

"What's so funny?" Juniper asked.

"It's mad corny."

"You're mad corny, so what's up? I wanna laugh."

"I was just thinking about how we got together."

"Mmmmhmmm."

"And what we'd tell our grandkids about how we got together."

"Grandkids?"

"Mmmmhmm, I said what I said."

Juniper bit her lip trying to suppress a grin be-fore speaking, "So what's the corny part?"

"The first thing that popped into my head to explain how we got together was started from a selfie, now we here."

"Baby," Juniper said, her tone quiet, but stern, "You can't ever say that to anyone else. In life. That's beyond corny...and I'm not having my life story summed up in a crib of a Drake lyric. A Drake lyric? C'mon Q."

"Not a fan of the Poutine Prince of Toronto?"

"Absolutely not."

"Hater."

"I'll be that," Juniper said, lifting her chin to brush her lips against mine.

If you enjoyed this book, please consider leaving a review on Amazon and/or Goodreads.
Keep up with my podcast #FallsonLove at:
www.nicolefalls.com
Follow me on Twitter:
www.twitter.com/_nicolefalls
Follow me on Instagram:
http://www.instagram.com/_nicolefalls
Like me on Facebook:
https://www.facebook.com/AuthorNicoleFalls
Join my Facebook Group:
https://www.facebook.com/groups/NicsNook/

Other Titles By Nicole Falls

Accidentally in Love Series:

Adore You

Smitten

Then Came You

Holliday Sisters Series:

Noelle the First

Brave Hearts

Standalone Titles

Sparks Fly

ABOUT THE AUTHOR

Nicole Falls is a contemporary Black romance writer who firmly believes in the power of Black love stories being told. She's also a ceramic mug and lapel pin enthusiast who cannot function without her wireless Beats constantly blaring music. When Nicole isn't writing, she spends her time singing off key to her Tidal and/or Spotify playlists while drinking coffee and/or cocktails! She currently resides in the suburbs of Chicago.

52607449R00067

Made in the USA
Columbia, SC
10 March 2019